Legend of the Wooden Star

Legend of the Wooden Star

Lee Allen

This book is a work of fiction. The names, characters, and events in this book are the products of the author's imagination or are used fictitiously. Any similarity to real persons living or dead is coincidental and not intended by the author.

Legend of the Wooden Star

Inspira Books Publishing LLC

Copyright © 2025 by Lee Allen

All rights reserved. Neither this book nor any parts within it may be sold or reproduced in any form or by any electronic or mechanical means, including information storage and retrieval systems, without permission in writing from the author. The only exception is by a reviewer, who may quote short excerpts in a review.

Library of Congress Control Number:

ISBN (hardcover): 9781662968370
ISBN (gift edition hardcover): 9781662968488
ISBN (french flap paperback): 9781662968495
ISBN (paperback): 9781662968563
eISBN: 9781662968501

Faith is searching for something that's not supposed to happen . . .

A miracle is when it does.

Prologue

The holidays had arrived, and Richmond was in the Christmas spirit.

Stores bustled with shoppers flowing in and out. People exchanging greetings not normally offered. Good cheer hung in the air. Even the downtown business district, filled with professionals dressed in lookalike suits and skirts, found it hard to ignore the festive mood. It was as if the smells coming from grandma's kitchen, offering aromas of holiday cooking, wafted through the streets.

Offices joined in the festive mood with various displays of good cheer—wreaths on office doors, office parties, and fellow workers exchanging gifts. Outside, even the modern high-rise buildings that crowded downtown, usually indistinguishable concrete, steel, and glass structures, now glowed with single strands of white lights running along their corners from street to roofline, then along the top. The effect created the illusion of a downtown filled with candles. The display even sent warm Holiday Greetings to travelers driving past the city along the outlying interstate.

That afternoon, while the sky turned an overcast grey, a weathered SUV traveled that same interstate. Approaching Richmond from the south, the SUV crested a hill. As it did, the downtown candlelit skyline suddenly loomed on the horizon. For the vehicle's occupants, a mother and father and their two grade-school children, the cheery spectacle did little to boost their spirits. Their third child, an eleven-year-old boy, rode in the ambulance directly to their front. The family had followed the ambulance for the past two hours, starting from their hometown in rural Virginia. The ambulance was headed to Richmond Children's Hospital, where their son was returning. His condition relapsed with his leukemia no longer in remission.

For the family, this Christmas was a reminder of another Christmas five years earlier, when their son was first diagnosed. He had been a first grader at the time, when they first heard what every parent fears ... The dark pronouncement that their child had cancer. That same specter now overshadowed this Christmas. Except this time, the news was even more dire. The leukemia's return was far more aggressive, the doctors explained. Their son's only hope, if he was to survive long into the New Year, was a bone marrow transplant.

Then, promising news just two days ago. The International Donor Bank found a perfect donor match in their system. Even now, the donor was being contacted to arrange for the transplant procedure. For the parents, it was an answer to a prayer, an offer of hope. Spying the spectacle of downtown lights, the mother turned to check on her two younger children seated in the back, where they occupied themselves with a video game. While she knew they understood that their brother was very sick, still they deserved a fun Christmas. But how that might happen now, as the family made their way to the Children's Hospital, she wasn't sure. She turned to study her husband, who was driving. She reached over and squeezed his shoulder. It was a gesture that said they were in this together. They exchanged a look that needed no words. All they could do, they knew, was face this Christmas with as much faith as could be mustered, knowing their only hope was a modern-day miracle.

Meanwhile, inside the cancer ward at the Children's Hospital, a resident pediatric oncologist frowned as she read the message that was just handed to her by the head nurse. It was an email that had come in from the International Donor Bank. The message was a heart-stopper. The donor, who had initially agreed to the transplant, reconsidered, and now no longer wanted to go through with the procedure. No reason given. None required. Donors were given complete anonymity and confidentiality about their decision to donate. The resident doctor knew that. She knew too that the young boy who the email pertained to was already on his way to the hospital.

She sighed. The news would be devastating to the family, who soon would be arriving. The resident was already aware of the critical stage of the boy's leukemia. She shook her head as she headed to another patient's room. It was the worst Christmas present she could imagine parents receiving. Once again, it made her question how a caring God could allow the heartbreak that she, as a doctor, so often saw on the ward. News like this was a reminder that she would never reconcile how a loving God allowed such needless suffering. It was what gave her purpose. The loss of her own little brother years earlier had motivated her to pursue medicine. Specifically, oncology. Someone had to defend and fight for these innocent children who were suffering. She was determined it would be her, with or without God's help.

Later that afternoon, a man dressed in flowing robes like those worn in the Middle East strode down the streets of downtown Richmond. He stood a head taller than most people he passed. Even his attire was in stark contrast to the other pedestrians bundled in winter clothes. Still, no one took notice of him. Reaching a modern multistoried hospital, he stopped and gazed upward, fixing his eyes on a certain window. For a long moment, he gazed thoughtfully. Finally, giving a satisfied nod, he turned his attention back to the street.

Legend of the Wooden Star

He was early for his rendezvous. Looking around, he decided to continue walking. It was an enjoyable time to get acquainted with the city. Up ahead was a street vendor. As he approached the vendor's cart, he heard the vendor hawking to passersby, "Get your Christmas ornaments! imported from around the world." He walked over to get a closer look. There was an assortment of ornaments dangling from the cart, clearly mass-produced. Some were factory-painted plastic ornaments, others were made of trinket gold and silver; they dangled from a wire running from post to post across the cart's front. One ornament caught his attention. It was an intricate Christmas star made of cheap gold metal, meant to adorn the top of a Christmas tree.

Seeing the tall stranger eyeing the star, the vendor pitched, "Hand-crafted in the Holy Land. Home of the first Christmas." Could he wrap it up for him, the vendor asked? The robed stranger shook his head no. The star he was looking for—he gestured solemnly toward the sky—was up there. With a confused shrug at the stranger's response, the vendor turned his attention to more promising prospects walking past. Again hawking, "Get your Christmas ornaments here! Imported from around the world!"

He continued down the street. Now realizing he was famished, after the great distance he had traveled to get there, he wondered if he might find a restaurant serving Persian fare. Just then, his keen nostrils picked up the aroma of roasted lamb. Following the source, he spied a food truck ahead advertising lamb kabobs. The aroma carried him back to the food bazaars of his home country. A smile broke across his face for the first time that day as he headed for the truck. As soon as he satisfied his hunger, he assured himself, he would turn his attention back to the reason he had come to Richmond. A mission he knew would require all his wits to succeed.

This time, he vowed, he would not fail. Not when the outcome determined another young boy's future. A boy whose life, even now, hung in the balance.

Chapter 1

Wednesday afternoon
The week leading into Christmas weekend
Richmond Children's Hospital

A group of college-aged young people filed through the double doors leading into the brightly decorated Children's Cancer Ward. They were members of a young adult singles Sunday school class, come to bring the children Christmas cheer. The head nurse welcomed their arrival.

"Hello, and thank you for coming today. I understand you're with a local community church across town. What a wonderful gift, to take your busy afternoon during the holidays to come visit our kids. The children are expecting you."

She lowered her voice. "As you might expect, many are fighting for their lives. But they always manage to wear a smile. It will warm your heart when you see."

The head nurse turned to another nurse. "This is Nurse Shelley. She will take you to meet the children. We understand you have come ready to decorate their rooms for Christmas. That's wonderful! We recommend you pair up in twos or threes to a room, so it doesn't overwhelm the children."

Hunter Reid, one of the class members, poked his girlfriend, Denèe, standing beside him with his elbow. She poked back playfully. Both knew they were automatically a designated pair. He studied her while listening to the nurse. He was thinking back to how they had first met. That was two months ago. She had just started attending his church, after her family moved to town. Hunter had noticed Denèe that first morning across the room—her constant smile while making new friends and strikingly pretty features of obvious mixed ethnicity.

It was during the usual Sunday morning social, before the group broke into separate classes. Denèe had noticed him staring and smiled back. That was all it took. Hunter had shot a beeline over to formally meet this new girl. Soon, he was sharing about the church's annual Christmas play. A play he had written and was directing this year. Right off, Denèe had asked if she could be a part of the production. After the first week of rehearsals working together, they were an item.

She looked over and saw that he was staring at her. Smiling, she nudged him to pay attention.

"Follow me, everyone," Nurse Shelley said, leading the group down a long hall. At each door, two or three students peeled off to follow the nurse into a child's room. Each group toted a bag with crafts to decorate. Then it was Hunter and Denèe's turn. The nurse got their names. Then, before leading them in, she quickly gave a heads-up. "Joey has received some disappointing news since he arrived. Don't be surprised if he's not very talkative."

Following the nurse into the room, they saw a boy lying in the hospital bed next to the window, staring outside. An IV ran into one arm. Other cables running from a monitor were attached to the boy. Someone, the staff or the boy's family, had placed a small Christmas tree strung with multicolored lights and bulbs on a nearby table. White sparkly cotton made to look like snow wrapped the base. Other than three small presents around the tree, there was nothing else that was Christmasy decorating the room.

The nurse went over, checked the monitor, then spoke to the boy.

"Joey, you have visitors. This is Denèe and Hunter. They've come with their Sunday school class to visit you and the other kids to help decorate your rooms for Christmas. I'll let the three of you get acquainted. Call the nurse's station if you need anything."

She gave the boy an affectionate pat, offered Hunter and Denèe an encouraging nod, then left.

The boy, who looked to be eleven or twelve, briefly turned his head to look their way, then returned his gaze to the window.

For a moment, there was an awkward silence. Then Denèe, tugging Hunter's arm, pulled them over to the boy.

Always the social one, she broke the ice. "So nice to meet you, Joey. Hunter and I have come to have fun with you. Like Nurse Shelley said, we brought Christmas decorations to make your room festive." She offered a big smile. "Sound like fun?"

The boy briefly glanced their way, offered a shrug, then turned back to the window.

Not deterred, Denèe continued, "Hunter, let's show Joey what we brought."

"Sure!" Hunter started pulling an assortment of dollar-store decorations from the bag, spreading them out on a nearby table. There was a string of Christmas trees with alternating candy canes to hang on a wall, a plastic garland of holly with red berries to display, a Merry Christmas banner, a string of colorful lights, and supplies for making handmade crafts.

Hunter held up the string of Christmas trees. "Joey, where do you think we should hang these?"

The boy again turned to look and muttered, "Anywhere, I guess . . ." Then turned his gaze back to the window.

Hunter and Denèe exchanged a look that said What do we try next?

Taking a different tack, Denèe reached for the poster board that was brought along for crafts. "Joey, while Hunter hangs the decorations, what do you say you and I make some handmade crafts?"

Suddenly perking up, the boy turned to Denèe. "Can we make a star?"

Denèe grinned. "Of course." She looked at Hunter, who gave her an approving nod that said Keep going.

"What kind of star shall we make?" she asked.

"A big star to hang there." He pointed at the window. "To remind me to keep looking for my miracle star."

That caught their attention. Hunter stopped what he was doing. "Did you say a miracle star?"

Joey nodded. "It's a rare star my friend Shaz says will appear in time for Christmas."

Hunter and Denèe exchanged another look. What the boy was saying was intriguing.

Denèe pulled a chair close to the bed to sit near Joey. "Tell us more about this star, Joey."

"I'm still learning, but my friend Shaz says it's a rare star that only appears every few hundred years. When it does, it's brighter than any star in the sky."

"Did he say why it's called a *miracle star*?" Hunter asked.

Joey nodded. "Shaz says it can bring my miracle." He paused. "First, I have to recognize the star when it appears, then believe in its secret message."

Joey had their attention. "What is the message?" asked Denèe.

"That part Shaz says I have to discover for myself. But he's going to help me know where to search for it in the sky."

What the boy was saying had their curiosity. "How did you meet your friend?" Denèe asked. "Is he from your hometown?"

"No, I only met him after I came here last week." Joey's face looked pained. "After I heard the news."

"What news?" Hunter asked.

Joey took in a deep breath. "My leukemia has come back. It's why I came back here to Children's Hospital. This time for a bone marrow transplant. Then I found out there is not going to be a transplant."

"Why?" they asked.

His disappointment was clear. "My donor match changed his or her mind. They don't tell me who my donor is—or was."

Denèe and Hunter shared a look of concern. "We're so sorry to hear that," said Denèe. "What happens now?"

Joey looked uncertain. "They keep looking. There's this International Donor Bank—that's who found my donor. So far, it's the only match I have. It's somebody from another country. That's what Dr. Ellie—she's my doctor—explained to my parents and me."

He rubbed his eyes, forcing back tears. "I really need a donor."

Denèe reached out, tenderly patting his arm. "Hunter and I are so sorry to hear that, Joey." She looked at Hunter, who nodded.

"That's why I have to discover the miracle star when it appears." Joey turned and gazed out the window, despondent. "I'm not sure I can see when it appears from here in my room."

"Can you go outside at night and look?" Denèe asked.

Joey shook his head no. "Dr. Ellie says I'm too vulnerable. I could catch pneumonia."

Denèe nodded; she understood.

Hunter was curious. "Joey, your friend, how does he know so much about this miracle star?"

"He's a stargazer."

That caught their attention. "Where's he from?" Hunter asked.

"Another country I've never heard of..." Joey scrunched his face, trying to think. "Persia, I think he said."

Hunter frowned, directing his comment to Denèe. "That's odd. Nobody uses that name anymore. Persia is the ancient name for modern-day Iran."

Joey's eyes brightened. "He looks like he's from a long time ago—the way he dresses."

"What do you mean?" they asked.

"He wears a fancy robe—like a sheik in the movie *Aladdin*. And he wears a fancy headpiece."

"Like a turban?" Denèe asked.

Joey shrugged. "I don't know that name."

"Who else at the hospital has met him?" Hunter said.

Joey frowned. "You don't believe he's real either!"

Denèe gave Hunter a subtle shake of the head. "We're not saying that, Joey."

Hunter explained, "I only was wondering if anybody else has met your friend. Dressed like that, he would catch a lot of people's attention here at the hospital."

"He told me he comes at night because he only wants to see me."

Denèe changed the subject. "While we're talking, let's get started making that big star, Joey."

He brightened. "Okay!"

Denèe reached for the poster board, magic marker, and scissors. "Now, how big is big?" she asked.

"This big." He spread his hands the width of his shoulders.

"Wow, that is big! Okay. First, we must draw it on paper, then cut it out. Do you want to do it?"

"Can you?"

"Sure. Then I want you to wrap it in foil, okay?"

He nodded.

She started sketching. "I'm going to give it four big points of light, then smaller ones in between, because this is going to be a bright star. Sound good?"

He nodded excitedly.

"And let's make the bottom point long, like the Christmas star that pointed the Wise Men to where baby Jesus was born."

"Shaz says they were stargazers like him."

Hunter, who was still hanging decorations, perked up. "What else does he say about them?"

"That he comes from religion. I forget what it's called."

Hunter's eyes grew wide. "Did he say they were Zoroastrians?"

Joey's eyes grew wide. "That's it! How did you know that?"

Hunter spoke to Denèe. "This is amazing. Joey, Denèe and I are part of our church's Christmas production. It's about the Wise Men, and it so happens that it's about a miracle star too."

Denèe added, "That's why we are quite interested in what you're telling us."

"You have a Christmas play about a miracle star?"

"You could say that," said Hunter.

They watched Joey's eyes light up. "Can I come?"

"That would be wonderful. Do you think your doctor will let you?"

His excitement left. "Probably not..." Then he was hopeful. "Can you ask my mom?"

Just then, there was a commotion at the door. Denèe and Hunter turned to see who it was and saw a woman walk in. She obviously was not a nurse or doctor, as she was dressed in street clothes.

"Ask me what?"

Without waiting for a reply, she walked over and offered her hand. "I'm Karen Haskins, Joey's mother."

Denèe responded first, "I'm Denèe and this is my boyfriend, Hunter. We're here with our church group."

She smiled. "I heard. That's wonderful of you young people to visit the children."

Denèe explained, "So, we've been with Joey to decorate his room. In fact, we are just finishing making a star to hang in his window while he looks for his miracle star to appear. Right, Joey?"

Joey gave a big nod.

Karen gave her son an exasperated look. "And telling your new friends about your make-believe midnight visitor?"

Joey frowned. "Mom, I'm not making him up. Shaz is real, and he does come visit me!"

"Okay, okay," she said, trying to calm him. "Let's not discuss that now." She shot Hunter and Denèe a look that said whatever the issue was, it was still unresolved. "These young people are here to cheer you up. Let's focus on enjoying their company."

Upset, he turned to gaze out the window again.

Sighing, his mother turned to Hunter and Denèe. "Can we speak a minute out in the hall?"

"Of course," Denèe answered.

They followed her into the hall, outside of earshot for Joey.

"I don't mean to mix you up in this," she started. "I just spoke to hospital security. Now I'm about to speak with the floor's head doctor. My son has this idea that he is being visited by some stranger off the street, or from wherever. He comes late at night so nobody else sees him, so my son says."

She studied them, her face apologetic. "If it sounds unbelievable, it's because it is. Hospital security is replaying security camera footage to be sure. But I've been assured that nobody looking like the person Joey describes could walk through the halls, much less come onto this floor. Not without being seen and stopped. Especially at that hour."

Hunter spoke, "So, Joey's friend is imaginary? He seems to really believe he's real."

Karen nodded. "The hospital's psychologist feels it's a survival mechanism because Joey's chances for receiving a critical bone marrow transplant appear slim. His only donor has backed out. We learned that devastating news when we arrived last Friday."

Hunter and Denèe looked sympathetic. "We're so sorry to hear about your son's situation, Mrs. Hasklns," said Hunter.

Legend of the Wooden Star

She started to tear up. "I'm so sorry. This has put quite a strain on me and my family. Not just Joey's condition, but the strain to get here each day. We live two hours away, in south Virginia. Plus, Joey has two younger siblings who have to make the four-hour roundtrip."

"Why don't you stay in town?" Denèe asked.

"My husband, Al, just got laid off, so finances don't allow it. We tried to see if the hospital could help, but their accommodations for out-of-town parents is booked up for the holidays. The children are missing their friends, so it's just a lot."

She paused. "Anyway, concerning Joey and his imaginary visitor, please try to steer the conversation to something else. It's hard enough for him knowing he doesn't have a donor now. I don't want him even more depressed when he realizes his miracle star isn't real."

"We understand," Hunter and Denèe said together.

"Thank you. If you will excuse me, I have an appointment with Joey's doctor. I want to talk with her outside of Joey's hearing. I need to understand better what we are facing if a donor doesn't come through."

Joey gave a frown as Hunter and Denèe came back into the room. "I know my mom was trying to convince you that what I'm saying about my friend isn't true. That it's all just my imagination."

Denèe answered, "It's okay, Joey. Can your friend visit you during the daytime so everyone can meet him?"

"I already said that. Shaz says he only comes for me."

Hunter realized they needed to change the subject. "Denèe, let's help Joey finish his star so we can get it hung in the window."

Denèe held up the gold and silver foils for Joey. "Which one?"

Joey pointed to the gold foil. "Gold, so it looks like a real star."

"I agree." She handed him the foil. "Now your turn."

A minute later, the star was ready to hang.

"Perfect," said Denèe. "Hunter, can you help hang it?"

In short order, Hunter had it hanging from the ceiling in front of the window. The overhead vent blowing air made it twirl, causing the star to reflect light coming through the window. The effect excited Joey.

"I can't wait to show Shaz." A smile spread across his face for the first time today.

Hunter checked his Apple watch. "We gotta leave. Rehearsal is in an hour."

Joey looked disappointed. "Do you have to leave so soon?"

Denèe made a sad face. "Sorry, we do. But we want to come back to see you, if that's okay?"

Just then, Karen Haskins returned.

"Mom, I want to go to their church play. It's about a miracle star."

She looked genuinely surprised. "Really? You have a play about a miracle star?"

Hunter nodded. "It's the Bethlehem Star."

"Joey would love it," Denèe gushed. "It tells the Christmas story in a way no one has ever heard. From the perspective of a shepherd boy. Hunter wrote the script."

Karen Haskins offered Hunter an admiring gaze. "Impressive. And the play sounds wonderful." Then speaking to her son, "Joey, we'll have to see what your doctor says."

Joey frowned, then turned to look out the window again. "She's going to say no."

"He has no immune system protecting him right now," his mother explained.

Denèe tried to brighten the mood. "In the meantime, we told Joey we want to come back to visit."

Karen Haskins smiled. "That would be wonderful. Right, Joey?"

Joey turned from the window. "When can you come back?"

Hunter answered, "We'll try to come back soon as we can."

Denèe explained, "We have only two nights of practice left. Friday is the first live performance."

"That's exciting. Is there more than one?"

"Yes, every night through Christmas Eve."

"Do you play chess, Joey?" Hunter asked.

Joey frowned. "No."

"Would you like to learn? I can bring my set and teach you."

Joey beamed. "Sure!"

"It's a plan," said Hunter.

After saying goodbye and promising Joey to come back soon, Hunter and Denèe headed down the hall to the exit. As they passed by the nurse's station, Nurse Shelley stopped them.

"How did it go with Joey?"

"It was fun," Denèe answered. "Joey's a very sweet boy."

The nurse nodded. "He's special. Did he happen to mention his midnight friend?"

"As a matter of fact, he did," Denèe answered.

The nurse offered a sad look. "It happens. Especially with children. They have such strong imaginations. They can suspend reality. Unlike we adults. I told his parents that it's okay; Joey is just so wanting to get well and back to playing like any eleven-year-old." She offered a smile. "I'm glad you were able to cheer him up."

"Actually, we told Joey that we'll be back to visit."

"That's wonderful! See you then."

Nurse Shelley went back to work as Hunter and Denèe made their way to the parking deck.

Outside, the sun had sunk behind the surrounding buildings. The wind now whipped across the open parking deck, turning the already frigid air into biting cold.

"Brrrr, it's freezing!" Denèe pulled her coat up tight, bouncing up and down while she waited for Hunter to unlock her car door.

Hunter's vintage Volkswagen Beetle was a present from his father, Scott Reid, who drove it when he was Hunter's age. The classic Beetle. The car got its nickname for its bug-eye headlights.

Scott opened her door using a key, then ran around to the driver's side to do the same. Climbing in, he fired the engine and turned up the heat. "Sorry, it will take a minute."

"You mean it will take the entire trip," Denèe teased. "How do you stand it?"

Hunter grinned. "I'm used to it."

She snuggled down into her coat, pulling it up around her face. "Glad I came prepared."

As they pulled out of the parking deck, Denèe was pondering something. "What did you make of this strange visitor? Joey seems so convinced."

Hunter shook his head. "You heard what Mrs. Haskins and the nurse said about a child's imagination. And don't forget the hospital cameras at all the entrances and hallways. If someone showed up dressed like Joey described, the cameras would show him."

Denèe reluctantly agreed. "I just feel so sorry for Joey. What a disappointment about the donor. He seems so convinced, but if his visitor is make-believe, where did the miracle star come from? And his friend dressed in Middle Eastern robes and a turban. And don't forget, he didn't even know Persia was Iran's ancient name."

"Unless he got it from a Disney movie. He mentioned *Aladdin*," Hunter added.

"True. But the miracle star sounds like our play . . ." Denèe was thoughtful again. "Know what I think? We have happened upon a mystery. A Christmas mystery at that!" She looked over at Hunter. "I'm excited to visit Joey again. This whole thing has my curiosity going."

Hunter chuckled. "Mysterious hospital guest meets Nancy Drew."

She punched him. "I'm serious. I have a feeling there's something going on with all this. It's sounding too coincidental."

Hunter put the Volkswagen Beetle in drive and headed out of the hospital parking deck.

"After rehearsal, I want to stop by my grandparents' house. See if they have some thoughts about how to help Joey's family. Opa is in commercial real estate and knows a lot of people. Joey's family is having to make the four-hour drive every day. That's too much strain."

Denèe crossed her arms. "Are you inviting me to come along? I want to meet your grandparents."

Hunter offered a mischievous smile. "I was thinking maybe so. Plus, you haven't seen the book the play is all about."

Denèe got excited. "I've been wanting to see the book behind the play. Also, to hear the story of how your family came into the book. What you've told me sounds so mysterious."

Hunter nodded. "It is. Hey, are you hungry?"

"Famished!"

"Let's grab a quick bite before rehearsal. How's Chick-fil-A sound?"

She was still shivering. "No to-go. We eat in, where it's warm. Unless you want an assistant tonight who's an icicle!"

Chapter 2

Play Rehearsal
Westend Community Church

Hunter and Denèe drove straight to rehearsal after stopping for fast food. As usual, before rehearsal began, Hunter gave a pep talk.

"Okay, everybody, you have just two nights left to perfect your part. Tonight I want you to focus on the delivery of your lines."

The cast of thirty members nodded that they understood.

"Pay attention as Sheila Mae narrates. Everyone knows by now when it's time to speak. What's important is the smooth transition between narrative and action."

Again, nods.

"Okay, let's get in place for the opening scene."

Hunter jumped off the stage and took his usual seat three rows back in the auditorium. Far enough back to get the audience's perspective, while close enough to the stage to not have to holler.

While he waited for the curtains to open, his thoughts wandered back to when he first got interested in theater. It started when he was growing up, watching Westend Community Church's professional theater-quality productions. Both for Christmas and Easter. Even the church's sanctuary was designed like a commercial auditorium. Including professional lighting and sound. Even an orchestra pit.

Still, Hunter knew what initially got him attracted to theater. It was Penelope, the church's very own camel. As far back as he could remember, he had watched Penelope make her grand entrance into the sanctuary with a Wise Man riding atop. As a kid, he had dreamed of getting the role. Finally, it came at fifteen when he drew the lucky straw. The coveted role was so competitive that leadership had to resort to everyone having an equal chance, so there were no hurt feelings. Hunter smiled at the memory. When he rode Penelope that year, it was like being a celebrity.

Beyond his church's productions, Hunter had joined the drama club in high school. Then after graduation, he enrolled in the local university's theater arts program. And now, he found himself directing this year's Christmas production. But that had not happened by luck. Every year, Westend's director of music and special arts, Mr. Wilson, sought an original theme for

Legend of the Wooden Star

the Christmas production. Something different to keep people coming back.

"Can't disappoint our audience with reruns," he liked to say.

When Hunter had come across *Legend of the Wooden Star* on the bookshelf in his dad's old bedroom at Hunter's grandparents' home, he realized he had found a unique Christmas story for a play. It was a story that gave a first-person account of a shepherd boy who was present that first Christmas.

While called a *legend*, because there was no historical record, it still came off as believable. But more, it gave a deeper perspective of the dramatic events surrounding Jesus's birth. Events only briefly detailed in the Gospels.

When Mr. Wilson heard Hunter's idea to turn the story into a play, he was all in. Write the stage play, he tasked Hunter, adding that he wanted Hunter to be the director. A title Mr. Wilson always reserved for himself.

That was back in the spring when they had that conversation. Hunter at once went to work. By late summer, he had the play drafted. Mr. Wilson was thrilled with what Hunter had created, and production plans went into motion. Auditions for key roles were scheduled and costumes ordered. By late October, casting began.

The play's popularity made landing lead roles competitive. Auditions were held over two weekends, with several dozen people showing up to try out for the lead roles. Minor roles were easily filled by church members who didn't pretend to be actors, but who just wanted to enjoy being part of the play.

Hunter, Mr. Wilson, and Alice Gentry, another local teacher with stage experience in her background, had held the auditions. While giving preference to members as much as possible, Mr. Wilson insisted on acting ability and the right fit for each character role. Thus, more often as not, some roles went to thespians who worked at the local playhouses.

Final casting selections were made following the second weekend of tryouts. Except for the Magi servant's role, named Belteshazzar, no one fit the role for the lead character yet, Mr. Wilson had said, and Hunter had to agree. Notice was put out to local playhouses and the opportunity was put on the church's Facebook page. Meanwhile, Hunter had gone to his university's theater department for their talent resources. Still no success.

Finally, they had found a stage actor by vocation. A thespian who lived in Northern Virginia. He was even of Middle Eastern descent. Sahib, the actor's name, fit the part, but the logistics were not perfect. Sahib had a two-hour drive, which limited the number of times he could attend rehearsal each week. While his contract commanded a hefty fee, the church sold tickets to cover such costs. Besides, Mr. Wilson thought he was worth the price. Hunter had agreed.

With a full cast selected, rehearsals had begun the week of Thanksgiving. Meanwhile, church members were recruited to be part of the set crew to build the props under the leadership of Bob Dawson, a church member himself and a builder by profession. Bob had managed that job for several years running. Just as in the past, he along with Mr. Wilson, determined the type of set and props needed for each scene, then assembled his crew to begin construction. It was a major undertaking that was easily dismissed, except Hunter had watched the amount of time spent working by Bob and his team all of November.

By the first week in December, the sets and props were ready. With production seriously underway, rehearsals had increased to three times weekly and Saturday. Then two weeks out from opening night, rehearsals were upped to every weeknight plus Saturday and Sunday afternoons. It had been a grueling fall, for sure, but well worth it. Hunter knew being selected to direct a major production like this, much less before the age of twenty, was an honor.

All had gone smoothly, that is, until a week before the play went live, Sahib called to say he had to pull out. A family emergency in Lebanon required him to return to his home country. That news had thrown rehearsals into a tailspin. Filling the part had been a challenge from the start, and now with the show opening in a week, Hunter suddenly faced this unexpected crisis. Immediately, a frantic casting call had gone out to all the resources Mr. Wilson and Hunter could muster.

Then the oddest thing had happened. Two days after Sahib had broken his news, a Middle Eastern man had shown up at the church, explaining he had seen the Facebook posting that the church was seeking an emergency fill-in for a lead role in their Christmas production. That had been last Friday. Caelum, the man's name, had explained that he was in town on business through the holidays, had stage experience in his background, and would enjoy celebrating the season by being part of the church production. Mr. Wilson had taken one look at the man and scheduled him to come back the next day, Saturday afternoon, to audition.

Caelum had returned the next day as arranged. Hunter right off was impressed with Caelum's appearance, as had been Mr. Wilson. But the clincher was the audition itself. Not only was Caelum of Middle Eastern appearance and mannerisms, but his bearing, what Mr. Wilson called "stage presence," was captivating. Regal even. He was tall and his deep voice commanding, resonating with an authority, and he spoke with a cadence that was almost hypnotic.

Almost immediately, Mr. Wilson had leaned close to Hunter where they were seated in the audience watching and listening. They had their man. Hunter agreed. In fact, Hunter was exuberant after Caelum promised he could make practice every night. A detail that was critical with opening night just a week away.

From the first day Caelum joined the cast, rehearsals had gone off seamlessly. That Saturday, he had to, of course, read his lines. But by the next day, he had his lines memorized. Now what Hunter was observing was how, at every rehearsal, Caelum shared new interesting facts about the Biblical Wise Men—details about their positions in the king's court during the Persian empire, the influence the Old Testament had on the Zoroastrian priests back then, even astrological details that would lead them to seek out the Christ child.

Soon, all the cast members were engaged in hearing what Caelum had to share. It was amazing how quickly he had taken center stage as the unofficial authority on matters about the Wise Men. Which all made his showing up for the part, in Hunter's estimation, providential. Too mysterious to be by chance, was how Hunter described Caelum showing up. Either way, clearly Caelum was perfect to play the role.

As the first scene opened, Hunter focused on the stage. The shepherd boy, Micah, played by Hunter's old high school buddy, from the start was flubbing his lines. Frustrated, Hunter stood up.

"Stop! Josh, what are you doing? You still don't have your lines down? You have tonight and tomorrow night, then Friday you will have a live audience listening to you!"

Josh stopped speaking and gazed back out into the audience, squinting to see. Stage lights made it hard for anyone on stage to look out at the audience.

"Sorry, Hunter."

Hunter gritted his teeth. "What's going on?"

Josh shrugged. "My mind was somewhere else. I'm ready."

Hunter hoped so. Otherwise, they were in for a long night. "Josh, this is not the time for that."

A sheepish Josh nodded. "I'm ready."

"Okay, let's start from the beginning. Sheila Mae, read your last line before Josh speaks." Hunter sat back down and made himself relax.

Now, not five minutes into the scene, the radio mics worn by the actors started acting up. Crackling static made it impossible to hear the words.

"Everyone, stop!" Hunter turned to look up into the balcony where the sound booth was situated. He hollered at his sound man, "Wayne, what's going on with the mics?"

"Not sure," Wayne called back. "Tell Todd to speak into his mic again."

Todd, who played the angel who appeared to the shepherds, repeated his line.

Still crackling static. Even worse. This was no good.

"Give me a minute. I'll bring down another mic," said Wayne.

Up on the stage, everybody was starting to get antsy. Understandable. Rehearsal just started and there were already disruptions.

Wayne trotted down the aisle and climbed onto the stage. For a minute, he adjusted the mic on the angel costume. "Try again," he instructed Todd.

More static. Wayne removed the mic and clipped on one he brought down. When that didn't stop the crackling, he looked out at Hunter and shrugged. "I'm not sure what the problem is. Maybe have everyone turn off their mics and say their parts without sound while I try to find the issue."

Hunter nodded. "Everyone, this is a good time to focus on your delivery. Raise your voice and project."

Listening to everyone speak their lines without the mics made Hunter thankful for modern technology. He made a mental note. Tomorrow morning, he would ask the church office to call the company who serviced their audio. Just in case Wayne couldn't fix the issue.

Ten minutes later, the scene opened at the oasis. This was where the Magi arrived outside of Bethlehem in search of the Christ child. Hunter noticed that the palm tree prop that towered above the actors looked wobbly.

He saw that Denée was in conversation at the side of the stage with Bob Dawson, who managed the sets, including props. Hunter knew they were discussing the issue. Denée already told him her solution was to tie the tree off at the top using thin guy wires attached to the gang walk above the stage. The wires would be invisible to the audience, while insuring it didn't topple over. Hunter cringed at the thought of that happening during a live performance.

Denèe had become indispensable to Hunter. He wasn't sure how he would have managed directing had they not met a few weeks back and she joined as his assistant. The way Denèe anticipated a problem before it happened—like stabilizing the palm tree—had prevented numerous disasters.

Hunter thought about earlier, when they grabbed dinner. They had discussed the Haskins' situation of not having accommodations to stay in Richmond close to their son. But instead of having to make the long drive back and forth each day, he had decided right then that he would call his grandparents to see about stopping by after rehearsal. He wanted to share the family's situation. He was certain If anyone could help, it would be his grandfather Max Reid, a successful real estate developer.

Meanwhile, with the mic issue still unresolved and his mind on visiting his grandparents, Hunter was ready for tonight's rehearsal to be over. Tomorrow night's full-scale dress rehearsal would go better, he promised himself. Better to discover these issues now and fix them before Friday night!

Chapter 3

Following Play Rehearsal
Max and Ellen Reid's House

Ellen Reid checked her chili simmering on the stove. Taking a spoonful, she nodded, satisfied. It was ready for when her grandson Hunter and his new girlfriend arrived. Ellen had gone about making his favorite dish, chicken sausage chili along with fresh baked bread, after his unexpected call. He wanted to come over after rehearsal and would be bringing his girlfriend. Ellen had asked if they would be hungry. He had answered with an emphatic yes! Of course, she already knew the answer. When were young people not hungry?

During the call, Hunter had hinted that some strange things were happening that he wanted to share. That had piqued her curiosity. At the same time, she knew that was her grandson's style too. Whatever Hunter was involved with, he always made sure it dominated the family news cycle. Truth be known, Ellen enjoyed that part of his personality. Anyway, whatever this sensational news was that she was going to hear, she was happy just to be seeing him.

Lately, it had gotten harder to corner Hunter long enough to sit him down for a meal and visit. How long had it been since he last came over? She thought a moment. Two months? Other than Thanksgiving when he had popped in long enough to say hi, then popped out just as quickly to go meet up with his new girlfriend. Denèe was her name. Ellen didn't have much information yet but heard her family had recently moved to Richmond. Obviously, it didn't take Hunter long to recruit her help with the play. Ellen smiled at the thought. That was her grandson.

Recently, she had spied the two of them together from across the church sanctuary following the service, but before she could make her way over to say hi, they had left. Even so, she could see that Denèe was a pretty girl, of mixed ethnicity, curly black hair, light brown skin, and nice features. She looked to come up to Hunter's chin. But then Hunter was tall at just over six feet, like his father and grandfather.

From everything Ellen knew thus far, they made a nice couple. She had seen the church arts director, Mr. Wilson, the other night at church. He had gone on about Denèe's talents helping Hunter manage all the details surrounding the production. Clearly, she had a good head on her shoulders. Currently a high school senior, she had received early acceptance at William & Mary, no small feat, and had plans to pursue medicine, Ellen had heard. Hunter, on the other hand, was all about the arts, not the sciences. The two might one day head in different career directions, but for now, they were a good match, which made Grandma happy.

Ellen was proud of her grandson. Here he was at twenty, directing a big stage production. Even if it was being put on by their church. Still, she knew how it was a big deal, not just for Max and her, but the whole family. Ellen had made sure her circle of friends outside the church heard about the play too and that Hunter had written the play based on a story an unexpected guest had told Ellen, Max, and Scott, who had been a teenager at the time. It had been a memorable weekend, especially because Jenny had come out of her coma that Christmas morning.

There was something powerful about the story. A *legend* because, whether true or not, it was lost to history. Yet it was believable. Ellen was so proud of how Hunter had taken the story and turned it into a stage play for this year's Christmas show.

Her thoughts returned to the present. She glanced up at the wall clock in the kitchen. Hunter should be arriving any minute. He already had texted that they were on their way. She was expecting Max any time too. She already had alerted him that Hunter was coming for dinner. Max was busy these days developing a mixed-use township center out on West Broad Street. It was Richmond's famed street starting downtown and extending twenty miles into the outlying county of Goochland.

Over the years, the city had made a slow but steady expansion in that direction, gobbling up farms along the way, and turning them into shopping centers and housing developments. Max had seen it coming and secured land out there years ago, always saying time would bring opportunity in his direction. Now was not the time to retire, he told Ellen whenever she asked, hoping they could travel more. If anything, his real estate projects were keeping him busier than ever. She finally got him to commit to taking three vacations a year to go somewhere new. Two weeks each time. For now, she had to settle for that. Which made keeping up with her grandson Hunter and her two grade-school granddaughters from her daughter, Jenny, even more important than ever.

She heard the back door open. It was either Hunter or Max.

"Oma, we're here!"

It was Hunter. "I'm in here!" she called out from the kitchen. Untying her apron, she went to greet them.

At the back door, Hunter and Denèe were taking off their shoes, to not track in snow. Their coats were dusted with snow as well. Surprised, she looked out the glass storm door. "When did the snow start?" she asked.

Hunter was shrugging off his coat. "Sometime during rehearsal. It's not too bad out there. Not yet anyway."

Ellen put her hands on her hips, pretending to be upset. "My grandson finally has come to visit." She shot Denèe a wink to show that she was teasing.

"Wasn't I just here?" Hunter asked innocently.

"Like, two months ago! If your Aunt Jenny didn't bring over your cousins each week, I think I'd forget I was a grandmother," Ellen chided him good-naturedly. "I can't seem to even run you down at church!"

"Sorry, Oma, it's been crazy lately."

"I'm just giving you a hard time." She gave her grandson a hug. "I'm happy you could stop by tonight. I want to hear all about the preparation for the play."

Turning her attention to Denèe, she extended her hand. "I'm Ellen Reid, Hunter's grandmother, of course. You can call me Oma if you like. That's what my grandchildren call me. It's German for grandma." She smiled. "There's a story behind the nickname, but we'll save that for later."

Denèe took Ellen's hand. "Hunter talks about you all the time. It's nice to finally meet you, Mrs. Reid—Oma. I'm Denèe Myers."

Ellen scolded playfully, "Don't pay any attention. He exaggerates a lot!"

That brought a laugh from Denèe. "I can see already that we have something in common, Mrs. Reid—Oma."

Hunter frowned. "Okay, you two just meet and already I'm being ganged up on! Where's Opa? I need him for tag-team support."

Ellen laughed. "Your teammate is on the way. Here, let's get your coats hung up." She opened the hall closet, took Denèe's coat, and hung it. Speaking to Denèe, "I hope you like chili. It's Hunter's favorite."

That changed Hunter's mood. "Awesome, Oma. Thanks!"

"I do," Denèe answered. "Sounds perfect on a night like this."

Ellen nodded. "That was my thinking too. Okay, let's head to the kitchen. We can get acquainted there. I need to finish a couple of details for dinner."

Ellen's kitchen was warm and inviting, always with aromas of something cooking. It was a large, old-fashioned kitchen built by her father, a builder, in the 1950s. She and Max had moved into her childhood home in the nineties. While they could have remodeled and added a middle island and other updated features, Ellen preferred the old-fashioned, open kitchen design and had kept it that way. In one corner was a rustic oblong kitchen table that seated eight. She already had crackers and cheese, and Hunter's favorite, salted pistachios, waiting.

"You two take a seat and snack. Denèe, what would you like to drink? I have tea, sparkling water, and sodas—diet or regular."

"Soda sounds perfect. I can get it," Denèe offered.

Ellen pointed at the hall they had just come through. "They're in the refrigerator in the pantry. It's the door on the left in the hallway."

"Want one, Hunter?" Denèe asked.

Hunter nodded that he did.

Ellen wanted to hear how rehearsals were going. "Are you ready for opening night?"

Hunter, who was licking the salt off the pistachio shells before eating the nuts, made a face. "Not if tonight is any indicator. Josh Whitaker kept messing up his lines. This close to opening night! Then the radio mics that the cast members wear started acting up. Still don't know what that issue is. The church needs to get a technician to come out ASAP. Mics not working would be a disaster."

"For sure," Ellen agreed.

"Anyway," Hunter continued, "it's been one thing after the other. Last week, we lost one of our leading cast members."

"I didn't hear anything about that." Ellen frowned.

"He was an actor from out of town. Northern Virginia. Originally from Lebanon. Anyway, his family back there had a crisis, requiring him to fly back to his country. Just like that, I was without one of my lead actors."

"Wow! And at the ninth hour. That is a crisis. What did you do?"

Denèe had come back in with the sodas. "Hunter, can I tell your grandmother?"

"Sure, if you want to." Hunter went back to his pistachios.

"I want to hear, Denèe," said Ellen.

"Well, at first, it was a crisis, like Hunter said. From the start, we had trouble getting the right actor to play the part. Within a day after Sahib said he couldn't continue, out of nowhere, a stranger showed up at church. He had heard about the opening and wanted to audition. He turned out to be perfect for the part. Caelum's his name. He's Persian, so his appearance, voice, mannerisms, everything is perfect.

"But that's not all," Denèe continued, "Caelum knows all these amazing facts about the Wise Men from back then. They were a religious caste of priests. They were astrologers, star gazers, Caelum calls them, which is why they knew how to read the signs in Heaven about Jesus's birth. You should hear him. He's amazing to listen to."

"So, this Caelum is playing the Magi's servant?"

"Yes, how'd you guess?"

Ellen smiled. "I know the story. I've read the book the play is based on. It's been on Hunter's father's bookcase upstairs for years now. Ever since a special guest, who we entertained one Christmas long ago, left it. In fact, back when Hunter's dad, Scott, was about Hunter's age."

Denèe nodded, remembering. "Hunter told me about that."

"The servant character's name is Belteshazzar, as I recall," said Ellen.

Denèe nodded. "I keep telling Hunter there is something mysterious about Caelum. Not just his surprise showing up for the role. Not even all the amazing details he shares nightly with the cast and crew about the Wise Men. He even talks about the Old Testament Daniel—as if he knew the prophet. Caelum will be saying Daniel used to say this or do that." Denèe looked puzzled. "I mean, unless he's making it up, how would he know details like that?"

"Hmm," Ellen pondered. "I can see why you would say that."

"That's not the only strange thing that's been happening involving stars and Christmas," said Hunter. "Tell Oma about our visit to the Children's Hospital today. Our meeting Joey. How he's looking for a star that sounds so much like the play."

Ellen stopped what she was doing. This was getting interesting.

Denèe nodded. "So, this afternoon, Hunter and I, along with our young adult Sunday school class, visited the Children's Hospital. Specifically, the cancer floor."

Ellen was impressed. "What a wonderful thing for your class to do."

"It really was special. Not just for the children, but for us."

"That's how those things go," said Ellen. "You want to give a blessing and end up receiving an even bigger one back."

"Exactly." Denèe nodded. "That's how Hunter and I were feeling by the time we left today."

She continued, "So we were divided into pairs to visit rooms. Hunter and I paired, of course. The boy we visited, Joey, is there because his leukemia has returned. He's there for a bone marrow transplant."

"Which now is called off," Hunter added.

Ellen stared questioningly.

"His donor backed out at the last minute," Denèe clarified.

"How horrible," Ellen said, making a face.

Denèe agreed. "He's only eleven years old, too young to be dealing with the scary prognosis if they can't find a donor soon. We met his mother. She shared a dire picture for Joey and what her family is going through. She and her husband also have two small children."

Ellen shook her head sadly. "And all happening at Christmas."

"We're coming to the strange part now," said Hunter.

Denèe nodded and continued, "Soon after we got there and started putting up the decorations we had brought, Joey wanted to craft a star. That's when he started telling Hunter and me the strangest things. He started telling us about a stranger who comes to visit him late at night. After hospital visitation hours. In fact, after midnight. He says the man, who he calls his friend, came to visit the first night he arrived at the hospital, which was last week sometime."

Hunter jumped in. "Here's the strange part, Oma. The man, who is Middle Eastern, dresses in robes like an Arab sheik. Even stranger, nobody sees the man come or go. Not the nurses, hospital security, nobody."

"Like, who could miss him if he walked into the hospital looking like that?" Denèe added.

"For sure," Ellen agreed. "Why is he there? Did Joey say?"

"This is where it really gets strange. He's come to help Joey search for a special star known to bring miracles. Sound like anything else?"

"The play," said Ellen, her eyes widening at the realization.

"It's uncanny, Ms. Reid—Oma," said Denèe.

"Here's the thing," Hunter added, "nobody believes Joey. Not his folks, not the hospital staff."

"But the details he describes, Hunter and I agree, it just sounds so real. We asked him all sorts of questions."

"Like what?" Ellen asked.

"Like, where does this man say he's from?"

"Where?"

"Persia. But here's the thing. As you know, Persia is the former empire now called Iran. And Joey had never heard of either. Also, Joey is using words like constellations and secrets behind the movement of the stars and planets."

"Joey's mother thinks he's imagining it all because of the hopelessness of his situation."

"That's so sad." Ellen grimaced. "But if he is imagining it all, where do they think he's coming up with such details?"

"Exactly," Denèe answered.

"Yeah, something doesn't make sense," Hunter added. He had finished off the pistachios and now joined Denèe eating crackers and cheese.

"Make sure to save your appetite," Ellen cautioned. "I made a big pot of chili."

Hunter downed a cracker in one bite. "No worries there, Oma. Not with your chili!"

Ellen was quiet for a moment, digesting what she had just heard. "You know, what you are saying sounds a lot like what happened to us." She directed what she was saying at Denèe. "We had a stranger come visit us one Christmas too."

"That was when Hunter's aunt was a young girl in a coma? Hunter has told me parts of what happened. I'd love to hear the whole story."

"Hunter's grandfather, he goes by Opa, will definitely have to share the story—"

A noise at the back door interrupted what Ellen was saying.

"That's Max coming in now," said Ellen. "I want him to hear about this young boy and the strange goings on."

Max walked into the kitchen, his jacket covered with snow. He was a distinguished-looking man, with graying hair at the temples, sporting an athletic build that belied his sixty-seven years.

"Max, you're covered with snow," said Ellen. "Is it bad out there?"

"Getting that way. It's starting to stick on the streets. Hunter, you and your friend will need to be careful going home." Max turned to Denèe, offering her a smile. "Hello, young lady. I'm guessing you must be my delinquent grandson's girlfriend?" He gave a wink. "I'm Max. Or Opa."

Hunter grunted. "So much for my teammate."

Max frowned. "Gotta give you a hard time for never coming around these days." Max tried to look stern, but Hunter knew he was kidding.

"I've already given him a hard time about that, Max."

Max walked over and pulled Hunter out of his chair for a hug. "Good to see you still know where we live."

That made Hunter smile. "Oh, brother."

"Max, we've been getting acquainted while waiting for you to get here. I've got chili on the stove and bread in the oven. It's ready if you want to get out of your jacket and wash up. I'll start getting it on the table. We're eating in the dining room."

A half an hour later, between spoonfuls of chili, Hunter and Denèe had caught Max up on all the earlier conversation with Ellen.

"What do you think, Max?" Ellen asked after they were finished sharing.

"I think whatever is happening is more than just a boy's imagination. What you're telling me sounds too detailed to come from thin air. And like you said, he doesn't know about these details, like Persia, to make it up if he wanted. Which leaves a bigger question."

"What's that, Opa?" asked Hunter.

"Who is this man paying the boy a visit? Obviously wanting to do so in secret because of the hour. Someone needs to find out, instead of dismissing the boy. He doesn't sound like he wants to hurt the boy, but clearly the child is vulnerable if no one is watching these visits."

"What would you recommend they do?" said Ellen.

"Have the nurses check in often. Put a security person walking the floor for a couple of nights and see what happens."

Hunter listened, then nodded. "Makes sense, Opa."

"You'll find your answer in short notice."

Denèe pointed her question at Max. "What do you make of this special star Joey is talking about?"

Max pondered a moment. "Did you check to see if there is some kind of astronomical event due?"

Hunter looked at Denèe with a sheepish expression. "Why didn't we think of that?"

"Let me check." Denèe pulled out her phone. After a quick search, she looked up, surprised. "You're right, Mr. Reid. A rare planetary conjunction is due to occur this Christmas. Last time it happened was 800 years ago."

Hunter looked thoughtful. "That's probably what Joey's friend is talking about."

"If he's real," Max added.

"This is giving me goosebumps," said Denèe. "First, our play is about a special star. Then today we meet a boy looking for a special star. And now a rare astronomical event is about to happen that creates a special star."

Ellen looked at Max, impressed. "You sound like your favorite detective, Sherlock Holmes."

"Elementary." Max winked.

Ellen chuckled. She knew Max was referring to Holmes's classic response to Dr. Watson when he discovered a clue.

"How did you figure that out so quickly, Opa?" Hunter asked.

"Your grandfather is a shrewd man," said Ellen.

Max looked first at Hunter, then Denèe. "Now you need to answer the most important question."

Denèe answered. "Is Joey's visitor real?"

Max nodded.

Hunter turned to Denèe. "Tomorrow morning, let's call Joey's mother and tell her what Opa just said. Get hospital security involved."

"And what if this boy is telling the truth?" said Ellen.

"Then we have a real *Nancy Drew* mystery on our hands." Denèe smiled.

Hunter changed the subject. "One more thing, Opa. Joey's parents and siblings. Karen Haskins says they can't afford a hotel, so they make a four-hour round trip every day to see her son."

"Where do they live?" Max asked.

"Near South Hill on the border of North Carolina."

Max nodded. "That's a drive to be doing every day. Who are the siblings?"

"Two grade-school children. That's all we know," Denèe answered.

"Making matters worse, the father just got laid off," Hunter added.

"What are you thinking can be done?" Max asked.

"I was hoping you might have some ideas, Opa," said Hunter. "Being you're in real estate."

"I would think the Children's Hospital has some kind of housing available for families."

"Like the Ronald McDonald House?" said Ellen.

Max nodded. "Especially for a children's hospital. Did the boy's mother mention that?"

"Only that the hospital had nothing available. What housing they can provide is booked for the holidays. Mrs. Haskins said there was nothing available."

Now Max spoke, "My company renovates apartment buildings downtown near the hospital. First, I need to check to see if we have finished furnishing those units."

He smiled. "Assuming we do, I think I can work something out."

Denèe looked pleased. "That's wonderful, Mr. Reid."

"I would want to meet the parents, of course. What's their last name?" said Max.

Hunter answered, "Haskins. The mother's name is Karen."

"I heard her say her husband's name is Al," Denèe added.

Max nodded. "Okay. Once I confirm some things, I'll call you in the morning, Hunter, so you can arrange for me to meet up with them."

"Max, I have an idea. Let's have the family over tomorrow night for dinner. Early enough so Hunter and Denèe can eat and get to rehearsal on time. I want to meet the family and see how else they may need help. This has got to be hard, especially at Christmas. Can one of you contact the mother in the morning and see if they would like to come over for a meal? I'm thinking five o'clock."

Denèe nodded. "I'll call. She gave us her cell number so we could stay in touch. We were already planning to go back to visit Joey."

"Thank you, Denèe." Ellen smiled.

"You two had better get going soon," said Max, gazing out the dining room window. "Snow is still coming down out there. Hunter, you think your little VW can handle it? You can borrow my SUV."

"We'll be okay. The engine is in the back, which really helps for traction."

"Let me fix up dessert quickly. Is gingerbread with ice cream good for everybody?"

Twenty minutes later, they finished eating and were now said goodbye at the back door.

"We will plan to see you two again tomorrow night," Ellen said, giving them both a hug. "Denèe, it was so nice to finally meet you."

"I know now why your chili is so popular." Denèe smiled. "It really hit the spot."

Ellen gave her another hug. "So happy to see my grandson has such good taste."

"The real question is, does Denèe?" Max said playfully, giving Hunter a playful punch on the arm.

Denèe gave a chuckle. "Let's just say it's not his cold car I love!"

Everybody laughed at that, even Hunter.

Hunter snapped his fingers. "I just remember I promised to let Denèe read the original story in the book. Is it stil on the bookshelf in Dad's old room?"

Ellen nodded. "It's still there."

"Be right back," said Hunter, bounding up the stairs.

A minute later he was back downstairs holding the antique leather-bound book. He handed it to Denèe smiling. "As promised."

"I can wait to read the original story," Denèe said, examining the small book.

"Okay, let's head out," said Hunter.

"Let us know you both got home safe," said Max.

Ellen and Max watched from the door as Hunter and Denèe made a dash for his VW.

"Can't believe that little car is still on the road." Max laughed.

"You're the one who kept it stored in the garage until Hunter was of age," Ellen chided.

"True." Max shrugged.

Climbing in, Denèe shivered while Hunter scraped the windows. He had started the car, but of course, she knew there would be no heat for several minutes. And no seat warmer either.

Finally, Hunter climbed in. "Hey, it's warm in here compared to out there."

Denèe made a face. "Very funny. Next time I ride with you, I'm bringing a portable heater." She wasn't kidding.

Hunter offered a sheepish smile. "Just think about this summer when I can take the top down."

"Well, I may be in hibernation until then!"

Chapter 4

Late Wednesday Evening
Children's Hospital

It was midnight. The hallway on the cancer floor was so quiet, one could hear a proverbial pin drop. A single female nurse manned the nurse's station. Her duty was to monitor if a child called for help, which was unlikely as they were all sleeping. But one child still lay awake, refusing to doze off. It was Joey Haskins, waiting for his friend to arrive.

Just then, the door opened. Joey's face broke into a smile. "Shaz, you're here!"

Shaz entered the room, his Middle Eastern robes swishing as he walked. Closing the door behind him, he came bedside and looked down at Joey with a pleasant expression. "My young friend, did I not say I would come?"

Joey was captivated by his friend's deep bass voice and accent. It was impossible not to listen. Shaz made each word sound important. Joey smiled. "Yes, you did."

Shaz noticed the gold foil star hanging in front of the window. "What have we here?"

"I made it to remind me to look for the Miracle Star that you said will soon appear."

"It's a marvelous star. You made it today?"

Joey explained, "Two college kids came by this afternoon with their Sunday school group to visit all of us here. I'm quite sure they were boyfriend and girlfriend. The boy helped decorate my room." Joey pointed to the walls displaying Hunter's handiwork. "The girl helped me make the star."

Shaz walked over to the window, then using his finger, flicked the star so it swung back and forth. He watched for a minute as it caught the light and reflected it back. Satisfied at what he was seeing, he turned back to Joey. "The Miracle Star is due to appear in just a few short days. I must help you to prepare for its special appearance."

"How do we do that?"

"I will bring my charts that show the movements of the planets and stars. They are ancient charts. You will need me to explain them, but once you understand the divine nature of the heavens and their language, you will see how they can reveal many secrets. That is, if a person is willing to seek out their wisdom."

"Wow! You mean the stars and planets can speak?"

Shaz's laugh echoed through the room. "The Universe, as it is known today, is both deep and wide.

Legend of the Wooden Star

Looking up into the sky at night, how can one not help but want to discover what the Universe has to say?"

Joey's expression was eager now. "I want to discover."

Shaz smiled. "What is important to understand, my young friend, is that heaven reveals its secrets to those who are willing to look for the answer. Then once revealed, that person must then believe to receive."

Joey frowned. "I don't understand. How do I do that?"

Shaz, towering over Joey, smiled again. "First, you must earnestly search for the star to appear. Then, most importantly, understand its meaning hidden from the casual observer."

Joey finished Shaz's thought. "Which is to, first, seek."

"Ahh . . . you are a bright boy, as I suspected."

Joey scrunched up his face. "I'm not sure how to seek."

Shaz laughed again. He seemed to enjoy laughing. He placed his large hand on Joey's small shoulder, giving him an affectionate squeeze. "Do not worry, my little friend, that is why I am here. I will teach you."

"I'm glad you're here to help me." Joey was thoughtful. "But why seek an answer in the stars?"

"It is where the Creator has displayed his mysteries from the beginning of time. The movement of the stars and planets is the language of the Universe. That is why, where I come from, we diligently study and look for clues that will answer our questions. For now, just remember the order of things."

"First, I must seek my miracle. That's why you will help me look for this special star to appear . . . I think I am beginning to understand."

"I can see that you are." Shaz gave him an affirming nod and turned back to the window, gazing out into the darkness. "Where I come from, we believe an invisible hand guides all, to include the stars and planets as they move across the heavens. Why would the Creator not speak through his creation? Of course he does. We are mere mortals. We cannot control much beyond ourselves. That is why we must look outside of ourselves for answers to important questions. The stars do not dictate; they only can reveal."

"So, what is important about this special star?"

"Ahh, now you are asking the right question. The appearance of a special star is a sign meant to reveal the timing of an event. When it appears, it is of great significance. Especially when such an occurrence is rare. But these are mysteries only true seekers ever discover."

Legend of the Wooden Star

Joey gazed at his tall friend still facing the window. Shaz reminded him of a wizard—the strange clothes and his words that sounded so wise, like a wizard. In fact, the word *wizard* to Joey sounded like it came from the word *wise*. Even Shaz's eyes were hard to stare at, as Joey felt like Shaz was reading his thoughts.

"My mom talked to the hospital people today. She said no one sees you come or go from my room, so they don't believe you are real."

"But you do?"

"Of course, I'm talking to you now."

"You see. You don't doubt I'm here. In the meantime, the others don't believe I'm here. Who do you think is right?"

Joey brightened. "Me, of course. You're here. But how come they don't see you? Are you sure you aren't a wizard?"

"Well, I do have some of those traits. You see, it is important for us to discuss these issues alone. People who do not believe will weaken your own belief."

"That makes sense."

"But enough conversation. I brought something for you to entertain yourself with while you wait for your miracle. Do you like board games?

Joey's eyes lit up. "Sure!"

Shaz drew something from his robe. It was a long scroll, like a piece of leather, rolled tight. Untying a leather lanyard, he unrolled the scroll onto the tray table. He laid it out flat to reveal checkerboard-like squares, the pattern etched into the leather. Next, he pulled out two small leather bags and emptied their contents onto the tray table. One bag held dark-colored stones, the other light-colored.

Shaz pulled a chair up to the opposite side of the tray table from Joey. "This is a game for two players. Pick your color stone."

Joey picked the brownish stones. "What kind of game is it, Shaz?"

"It is like your chess game today. But this game is ancient, going back more than 2,000 years. It was quite popular back then with merchants and soldiers who traveled across the vast Roman Empire. The game was called *Ludus Latrunculorum*.

Joey made a face. "Ludus what?"

Shaz chuckled. "It's Latin. Translated, it means 'Game of Mercenaries.' Like chess, the goal is to outwit your opponent until he is captured."

Joey brightened. "My friend Hunter, who visited today, promised we would play chess when he comes back next time. Is this a hard game to learn, like chess?"

Shaz's eyes danced with mirth. "Not for a smart young boy like you."

For the next number of minutes, Shaz explained the rules, patiently showing Joey different moves and strategies.

Finally, Joey looked up at his friend. "Okay, I think I understand."

"Then let's begin a game."

For over an hour, they practiced, with Joey losing several games. Frustrated, he said, "I'll never beat you, Shaz."

"You are a valiant opponent but still learning. You must give yourself time."

Joey yawned. "Can we play again tomorrow night?"

"Of course. I shall leave the game with you to study. Perhaps when your friend comes, you can teach him to play as well."

Joey nodded as he closed his eyes. He was fast asleep before Shaz left the room.

Chapter 5

Thursday, early morning
Joey's hospital room
Nurse Shelley discovers the game

Nurse Shelley had just come on duty. She had first shift today, starting at six o'clock. Her first task was to make the rounds, checking on the children—see who was awake, how they were feeling, what they wanted for breakfast, and always check their monitors.

There was an assortment of cancer-related conditions on the Hematology and Oncology floor, from children who were in recovery, after various cancer treatments, to those who were in the final terminal stages, where medicine could do no more. Nurse Shelley considered her profession to be a special calling, working in oncology. Children were too innocent for this to happen to them. Many hardly had started life and now faced the prospect of not living. Sometimes this job was emotionally tough. She got attached to a child, only to often have to say goodbye. At times, Shelley wasn't sure how she could continue doing that.

Lee Allen

Joey Haskins was one of those children you couldn't help but get attached to. Yet she knew his condition was now dire. She smiled just thinking about him. He was a naturally curious boy, serious but at the same time often funny. Sometimes she would come, and he would pretend to be asleep, refusing to wake when she nudged him. Then suddenly, he would open his eyes and giggle. It had gotten to be their game. She had a feeling it was a diversion because he was bored.

Joey had arrived less than a week ago, but already the nursing staff was enamored with him. He was always asking questions, wanting to know what they were doing to get him well. Yes, he knew his donor had backed out. That had been a tough blow. Sometimes, when he didn't know she was looking, she would walk past his room and see him staring out the window, solemn.

The important thing now was all this ruckus about a visitor, who Joey claimed came to see him in the middle of the night. Was he just imagining it? The staff was convinced so. Footage from the hall cameras showed nothing. After visiting hours, no one could be seen in the hallways. Much less someone dressed in robes, like Joey claimed his visitor wore. In fact, Joey's story sounded so fantastical that no one gave his claim serious consideration. Understandably, he was frustrated that no one believed him. Nurse Shelley decided from the start to avoid the subject. As far as she was concerned, it wasn't hurting anyone that Joey was imagining this visitor, so why make it an issue?

This morning, the head nurse had wanted Shelley to head straight to Joey's room to check on him and see if it looked like anyone had been there during the night. Already, the third-shift overnight nurse had reported no incidents. No visits by strangers anywhere on the hall. Still, just to be sure, before Joey's parents arrived this morning, the head nurse wanted an updated report. At this point, she wanted to make sure they were covered, especially because the Haskins had elevated this to the hospital's top administrator.

Arriving at Joey's room, she saw that the door was closed. Odd. Usually, the children's doors were left open, especially at night when the floor was quiet and the children were sleeping. She cracked the door and peeked in. Joey was still fast asleep. She had noticed he was sleeping in lately. As if he had stayed awake late. The room was still. No one there, of course.

Then something sitting on the tray table caught her attention. Curious, she went over for a closer look. It was a flat piece of leather covered with painted or etched squares; she wasn't sure which. Smooth round stones, one set dark, the other light, lay on the board, playing pieces. It was some kind of game. Surely not modern, as it looked too primitive. The leather board was old. Ancient even.

"What in heaven's name," she muttered under her breath. She glanced over at Joey. He was still asleep.

Whatever it was, she had a feeling that it showing up in Joey's room was about to set off alarm bells all the way to top management. Just then, she felt the compulsion to look around the room. Just in case someone was still there and she hadn't noticed. No, she saw that the room was empty. No one except her and Joey. The bathroom door was open. She cautiously peeked in. Empty. She felt relieved.

This needed to be reported immediately. Feeling her heart race, she hurried out of the room and headed straight to the nurse's station. Whatever was going on, her gut said that a peaceful morning was about to turn into pandemonium. She was sure that the head of security was about to get involved, perhaps even corporate. She made a mental note to keep all the details fresh in her mind.

Now she thought of Joey's parents. What would they say? What would any parent say with something inexplicable like this happening to their child? The exposure to liability for the hospital was huge.

Fortunately, nothing bad happened. Still, she had a feeling this was not going away. The thought of no one believing Joey struck at her heart. She smiled. At least now the adults had to believe him!

Chapter 6

Later Thursday morning
Westend Community Church
Hunter learns that the Game of Mercenaries
was found in Joey's room

The snow had stopped sometime during the night. Now what remained on the ground sparkled in the dazzling sunlight. Even so, Hunter wasn't paying attention to the weather as he made his way to Westend Community Church. Instead, he focused on his to-do list before tonight's full-dress rehearsal. Pulling into the church lot, he parked close to the office building, climbed out, and trotted inside. His first order of business was to get the office to call the company that serviced the church's audio system and let them know the remote mics were malfunctioning.

"Tell them it's an emergency work order," Hunter urged the church secretary, Janice Winslow, after filling her in on what had happened at rehearsal.

"I'll make sure to emphasize that it's an emergency," she promised, looking up the number.

"And make sure they understand that tomorrow night is our opening performance."

She paused and studied Hunter. "Are you nervous? Tomorrow night's a big night." She gave him a motherly look. She was Hunter's mother's age. The two were good friends.

"Yeah, I'm starting to feel the butterflies," Hunter admitted.

"Are your folks coming for opening night?"

Hunter shrugged. "They won't say."

She smiled. "They probably don't want you thinking about them in the audience. Not the first night."

"I think you're right, Mrs. Winslow."

He pointed in the direction of the Arts & Music building. "I'm meeting up with Miss Cho, our costume designer. She's organizing all the different outfits for tonight's dress rehearsal."

"Go do your thing. I've got you covered on the service call. I will let you know what they say," she promised.

Hunter thanked her and headed to the Arts & Music building. Inside, Miss Cho, an elderly Korean woman, was there with two of her young seamstresses, also Korean. They were busy sorting through boxes, separating costumes by character.

Miss Cho held the official title of Costume Designer for the production. Mr. Wilson insisted on crediting key positions with the titles customarily used for film and stage. Even though it was a church production, he still insisted it was a professional performance. Hunter admired that about Mr. Wilson. It was what made the church's productions special.

Seeing Hunter walk in, Miss Cho offered a quick bow. "Good morning, Mr. Director."

Hunter bowed back. "Good morning to you, Ms. Costume Designer. "How are we looking? You finding everything?"

She held up her clipboard for him to see. "'Major costumes all here." She had check marks beside the major characters and their specific apparel, including the minor roles. Hunter knew there were costumes for sixty people. Many were just fill-ins for the crowd scenes, with no lines.

He scanned the room. Scattered everywhere were boxes of all sizes. He couldn't imagine figuring out what went where. Walking over to several large boxes, he looked inside. They were filled with an assortment of different costumes that still needed to be sorted. The contents ranged from the everyday apparel worn by ordinary Jewish citizens back then to Roman soldier uniforms to tunics and royal robes worn by Pilate, the Magi, plus the religious robes worn by the Pharisees and Sadducees. All the costumes accurately depicted Palestine in that day. Plus, there were headpieces, costume jewelry, swords, spears, shepherd staffs, and all the various props. In a corner, he noticed a cross leaning against the wall. It was a poignant prop that didn't naturally fit into a Christmas story. Except in *Legend*, it did.

"I'm glad it's you and not me figuring out where everything is," he chuckled.

"I do the same every play. Miss Cho knows her job." She always spoke matter-of-factly in her Korean accent.

"Yes, you do," he agreed.

Hunter had not been involved in the task of going through catalogues and ordering the various costumes to be used in the play. That had been carried out under Mr. Wilson's direction. He wanted Hunter focused on running the rehearsals and directing the cast. That was more than a full-time job, he had told Hunter early on. Mr. Wilson wisely had been correct about that.

Then last week, while going over production details, Mr. Wilson had shown Hunter a tally of the costume invoices. The dollars spent were jaw-dropping, in the thousands. Hunter had no idea before seeing the tally. Fortunately, ticket sales had exceeded the cost to produce the play, Mr. Wilson had said. While a church was nonprofit, still it had to operate in the black, like any business. Or be out of business!

Legend of the Wooden Star

He spoke sincerely, "Thank you, Miss Cho, for coming in this morning, and please thank your assistants."

"No worries; we are ready for tonight."

Just then, Hunter's cell rang. It was Denèe. She had gone with her mom to do some Christmas shopping this morning.

"Hey, did you talk with Mrs. Haskins yet?" he asked.

"Just now, she called me back. I had left her a message a couple of hours earlier." Hunter already knew Denèe had promised his Oma she would call to invite the family for dinner tonight.

"Are they coming?" he asked.

"I didn't have a chance to ask her."

He didn't expect that. "Why not?"

"Wait till you hear what happened."

He suddenly felt a lump in his throat. "Tell me! is Joey okay?"

"He's fine. Nothing like that. You know the midnight visitor Joey was telling us about?"

"Of course. We've been talking about it ever since." Hunter was starting to get impatient.

"Turns out, the visitor friend of his is for real!"

"What! How do you know?"

"Nurse Shelley, you remember from yesterday, she found proof this morning. Wait till you hear what."

"Tell me," Hunter said. He could feel his pulse quickening.

He heard Denèe take in a deep breath, trying to calm herself.

"You know the game the shepherds were playing that night around the campfire in the opening scene?"

"Of course."

"Well, that very game showed up in Joey's room this morning."

Had he heard right? "Say that again."

"It's the same game. Karen Haskins called it the Game of Mercenaries. It's what Joey is calling it."

Hunter felt a tingling sensation creep up his neck. Something very strange was going on. Unbelievable. "Denèe, how could that even be?"

"I agree. You're still at the church, right?"

"Yes."

"We need to get down there and find out for ourselves what is going on. I'm heading to the church now. My GPS says I'm thirteen minutes away. See you then."

She hung up before he had a chance to say anything else.

Legend of the Wooden Star

Hunter strained to think. Whatever was happening had all sorts of implications. He tried to think through them. One thing he felt was certain; it wasn't coincidence. Those odds were too long. But then that opened even more questions. Denèe was right; they had to get down there and find out for themselves what this all could mean.

His attention was drawn back to Miss Cho and her girls working. He noticed that she kept looking over at him.

"You look like you've seen a ghost," she said.

He made a face. "You're close, Mis Cho. Something has come up. I gotta go! Sorry. Are you good without me here?"

"Everything's fine. You don't do anything anyway." She offered him a teasing look.

He laughed. "You are probably right. If I'm not back before you finish, see you tonight." He gave a wave and headed to the parking lot to wait for Denèe.

Chapter 7

Thursday, late morning
Children's Hospital
Everyone knows that Joey's friend is real

Arriving in downtown Richmond, Denèe pulled off Broad Street and into the Children's Hospital parking deck. She had insisted on driving her car, saying Hunter's car was too cold. Hunter didn't mind. It gave him a chance to review his to-do list that he kept in the Notes app on his phone. Parking, they made their way into the hospital, then caught the elevator up to the Oncology and Hematology floor. At the end of the hall were the double doors leading into the cancer center.

The first thing they noticed was uniformed hospital security staff gathered around the nurse's station. Along with security, there were several others in business suits. Hospital management? Hunter and Denèe exchanged a look. They were thinking the same thing. Clearly, the news about Joey's visitor being real had the hospital rattled.

"Hunter, there's Nurse Shelley," Denèe said, giving a wave to the nurse.

She saw them and walked over. "Have you heard the news?"

They nodded.

"I talked with Joey's mother earlier," Denèe explained, "that's why we're here."

"Can you believe it?" The nurse's eyes were round with wonder.

"It must have everyone talking," said Denèe.

"The whole hospital."

Hunter pointed to the group huddled at the nurse's station. "Is that what they're discussing?"

Nurse Shelley pulled them aside, out of earshot. "Yes, hospital big brass all the way to the top is involved now. I was the one who discovered the game in Joey's room this morning when making my rounds. Since then, it's been crazy!"

That got Hunter and Denèe's attention. "Wow! What was your reaction?"

"I knew immediately that something very strange was going on. Just looking at that game, it was too odd-looking to not mean something was up. Sure enough, Joey told me it was his middle-of-the-night visitor who brought it."

She paused and took in a deep breath. "All along, what that young boy has been trying to tell us turns out to be true." She looked from Denèe to Hunter. "Honestly, I feel bad. But who could have imagined? It all sounded so far-fetched. I mean, a stranger coming and going and nobody seeing him?"

She paused. "If you can believe Joey, and I think we all do now, this mysterious friend of his dresses as if he's some kind of Middle Eastern sheik or prince. Anybody looking like that would stand out in a crowd, much less walking through a hospital in the middle of the night! They're talking now about posting a guard at the entrance and putting up cameras."

Nurse Shelley drew in close to them, secretive-like. "You want my opinion, security won't work. I tell you, there's something else strange that's going on. I can feel it."

Hunter and Denèe exchanged a look. "What are you saying?" asked Denèe.

The matronly Black nurse shrugged. "Just my opinion. I don't want to say anymore. Go talk to the boy and see what you think."

"Is Joey's mom still here?" Denèe asked.

"Yes, she and Joey's father are with him. I should warn you: Mr. Haskins is roaring mad. Understandable, if you think about it. Their son being visited by nobody knows who."

"Is it okay to go back there?" they asked.

"Of course, you're friends with Joey now. He hasn't stopped talking about you since yesterday."

They thanked the nurse and headed to see Joey. Reaching his room, the door was ajar. Peering inside, they could see Joey's parents, and Joey was sitting up in bed playing with his new game. Karen Haskins saw them first, then put her finger to her lips, making a hush signal, and walked over.

"Hi," she said in a soothing voice so Joey couldn't hear, "let's talk out in the hall."

Turning to her husband, she motioned for him to join them.

Out in the hallway, Karen made the introductions. "Al, this is Denèe and Hunter. They're the young people who visited Joey yesterday." To Denèe and Hunter, she said, "This is my husband, Al, Joey's father."

Al Haskins offered a nod in place of a smile. His face was drawn. He was wearing a two-day-old beard and clearly looked agitated, like Nurse Shelley had said. "Guess you heard about what's been happening?"

Denèe answered, "Yes, sir. Mrs. Haskins told me on the phone. Hunter and I wanted to come straight down."

"Please call us by our first names," Karen prompted. "The other is just too formal for Al and me."

"Okay," Denèe and Hunter agreed.

Karen explained to Al, "Joey was telling Denèe and Hunter yesterday all about his stranger friend who visits him."

"Yes, he called him Shaz," Hunter added. "Denèe and I were just now talking with Nurse Shelley. She's the one who discovered the game this morning."

Karen gave a pained look. "I feel so bad now, not believing our son." She looked over at Al. "He was trying to tell us, but it sounded so far-fetched."

Al scowled. "I blame the hospital. They should know who is coming and going. Lax security is what it is. They should be sued for allowing strangers to visit children unsupervised in the middle of the night! The only way we found out that he's for real is the game."

"That's the other thing," Karen said. "It's such an odd gift. When you see it, you'll agree. It looks like something out of a museum. Certainly not something you'd think to give a young boy."

Hunter and Denèe exchanged a look. It was time to explain. Hunter began, "This game is the reason for us coming. There's something else very strange that you should know."

Karen and Al stared at Hunter, not sure what he meant.

"Denèe and I are familiar with this game."

"You've heard of it before today?" Karen asked.

Denèe spoke, "It is ancient, like you said. It dates back to Roman times when soldiers and other travelers used to play it for entertainment while traveling across the Roman Empire. Hunter and I know about it because the game is in our church play."

"Church play?" Al asked, confused. "What's that have to do with anything?"

Karen explained, "Al, Hunter and Denèe are involved with their church's Christmas play. They were telling Joey all about it yesterday. Now Joey is excited and wanting to go see it."

"He can't go. He's too sick."

"I said that too." She looked back at Hunter and Denèe, her eyes widening, "You're saying this Game of Mercenaries is in your play? How odd."

"That's what we can't figure. How this stranger happened to give Joey this game, of all games. It just defies coincidence."

"What are you thinking then?" Karen asked.

"We don't know what to think. That's why we came," Hunter answered.

"We've never actually seen the game either," Denèe added. "Only read about it in a story the play is based on."

Al's eyes narrowed suspiciously. "I hope this isn't some kind of prank. You two really have no idea who this midnight visitor could be?"

"Really, we don't know any more than you," Hunter and Denèe said emphatically.

Hunter added, "There's something else strange. Yesterday, Joey was telling us about a special star his late-night visitor says holds the key to his miracle. Well, that's the theme of our play too. So, you can see why we are so trying to understand what is happening."

"This all doesn't sound possible," Al growled. "Somebody is orchestrating all this for why, who knows, but our son is deathly ill, and that's no funny matter. I'm going to get to the bottom of this."

Karen put her arm around her husband's waist. "All this is putting a strain on us. You can understand."

"For sure," Hunter and Denèe agreed.

"We're on your side, Mr. Haskins—Al," Hunter assured the couple.

"Do you mind if we visit with Joey for a while?" Denèe asked. "See what we can learn?"

"We want you to," Karen answered. "Joey will be so excited. You can find out something we don't know."

She looked at Al. "Let's let these two spend some time with Joey without us here. We'll pick up the kids from the hospital daycare and go to lunch." Looking at Denèe and Hunter, she said, "Will you be here when we get back? We'll be gone about an hour."

Hunter looked at his Apple watch and frowned. "Not sure. We have full-dress rehearsal tonight. Tomorrow night is our opening performance. I've gotta get back to the church."

"Hunter's directing the play," Denèe added for Al's benefit.

Karen smiled. "It all sounds exciting."

"It is." Denèe nodded.

"Okay, see what Joey has to say. I have a feeling he will tell you more than he tells us."

Karen stuck her head in the room and told her son they were getting lunch. "I'll let you surprise him." She smiled at Denèe and Hunter.

Denèe suddenly remembered. "Yikes! I almost forgot with everything that's happened. I called you this morning to invite your family to dinner tonight." Denèe quickly explained the invitation from Hunter's grandparents.

Hunter added, "Last night we were telling them about how you are traveling back and forth to see Joey. My grandfather, whose company manages a lot of real estate, has furnished apartments near here."

Al Interrupted, "Thank you, but we're doing okay."

Karen placed a hand on her husband's arm. "Al, I explained our situation to Denèe and Hunter when they were here yesterday. They know you were laid off and the hardship it's causing us."

"The apartment won't cost you anything," Hunter quickly added. "My grandparents just want to help."

For a moment, the couple stared, unsure how to answer. Finally, Karen, wiping a tear away, silently voiced a thank you.

"The Reids, that's Hunter's grandparents, would really like to meet you," Denèe added, offering an encouraging nod.

"And you can discuss the accommodations and see if they will help," Hunter added.

Karen looked at Al, who finally nodded. "Okay."

"Hunter and I will be there too. Here, I'll text you their address." Denèe took out her phone and began typing.

"We'll see you there then," said Karen, taking Al by the arm and heading down the hall.

"Can't wait to check out this game," Hunter said, unable to hide his excitement any longer.

Seeing them walk in, Joey's eyes lit up. "You came back! Come see what my friend Shaz brought me."

The game was set up on the tray table and positioned over the bed, so Joey could easily reach the pieces. Just seeing the game gave Hunter a shiver. It felt strange knowing what he knew about the ancient game and now seeing it in the most unlikely of places. With an eleven-year-old boy in his hospital room. Much less how it got to be there . . .

"Shaz says it's a lot like chess. I'll teach you."

"Sure." Hunter smiled at Joey. "Give me a minute to check out the game pieces."

Hunter picked up one of the stones. It was irregularly shaped, worn smooth over time. He counted the playing pieces. There were sixteen dark- and sixteen light-colored stones. The leather board was what gave away the age. It was clearly ancient. The edges were worn and the checkerboard squares faded. He counted eight squares across and twelve squares deep.

Hunter pondered, So this was what soldiers and traveling merchants played while sitting idly by their campfires out on the Roman highways. A game of competition to occupy themselves. He felt the leather. Sheepskin. It was still supple, amazingly.

He looked up at Denèe, who was studying the game as well. "What are you thinking?"

"How this game looks old enough to be the one described in the play."

"You know the odds of that are impossible, right?" Hunter said.

She shrugged. "I'm not sure about anything at this point."

"True." Hunter had to agree.

"Do you know what Shaz told me?" Joey had their attention. "He said my game goes all the way back to the first Christmas."

Hunter and Denèe stared blankly at Joey. "He said that?" Hunter finally spoke.

Joey nodded.

Hunter felt goosebumps crawl up his back.

Joey challenged, "Are you ready to play?"

"Okay, let's do it!" Hunter pulled up a chair on the opposite side of the tray table.

"First, you need to know the names. The board is called 'the city,' and the pieces are called 'dogs.'" Joey giggled. "They're supposed to be soldiers."

"Shaz and I played a bunch of games last night, so I learned a lot." Joey went on explaining, "The goal is to corner each of your opponent's pieces and remove them until they're all gone. The first person to lose all his pieces loses the game."

Hunter listened as Joey went into the other rules, then some strategies. Finally, he said, "Are you ready?"

"I think so." Hunter gave Denèe a wink.

She could see that for the moment, he was more into the game's competition than any mystery behind the game.

"Okay, we'll start by placing each of our sixteen pieces on the first two rows, eight on each row. Then we start advancing."

A half hour later, after five games, Hunter leaned back in his chair. "You're a tough opponent." Joey had won three games to his two.

Joey grinned. "I told you, Shaz taught me a lot."

"Want to play him?" Hunter looked at Denèe.

She checked her phone. "I don't think we can stay." She looked at Joey. "We'll play later. I'm curious. Did your friend Shaz say how he came across this game?" She glanced at the relic.

"Just that it was a game he's had for a long time."

Denèe and Hunter exchanged a questioning look. The more they learned, the stranger this got. Hunter had a thought. "When you see your friend Shaz next, would you ask him if he has ever heard of a story called *Legend of the Wooden Star*?"

"Legend?"

Denèe explained, "The original book that Hunter used to write the Christmas play."

"I really want to go." Joey made a sad face and looked away.

Denèe patted his arm. "We want you to."

They got ready to go. "Don't forget to ask your friend," they reminded.

"Okay. When will you be back?"

Denèe answered, "Hopefully, this weekend."

Denèe gave Joey a hug. Hunter shot him a fist bump, then they left.

They both knew that there was still much to do before tonight's final rehearsal. Especially since it was the first time the cast would be dressed in their costumes. Before that, they would introduce the Haskins to Hunter's grandparents.

Chapter 8

Thursday, five o'clock
West Richmond suburbs
Dinner at the Reid's

Hunter pulled into Denèe's driveway. He was picking her up to meet the Haskins at his grandparents'. He gave the horn a toot, then waited for Denèe to come out.

Now he replayed the day. After leaving the hospital and seeing with their own eyes the Game of Mercenaries, Denèe had dropped Hunter back off at church, then headed to meet her mom and finish Christmas shopping.

Back at church, Hunter had heard the bad news. The earliest that a sound technician could come was Tuesday, the day after Christmas. Now Hunter was anxious to introduce the Haskins and get to church. At this point, he could only hope Wayne could figure out the problem.

He checked his Apple watch. The Haskins were due at his grandparents' in fifteen minutes. Denèe came out the front door, waved, and gingerly negotiated the front sidewalk to avoid ice.

She climbed in, leaned over, and gave him a quick kiss. "We're about to be late," she said, breathing hard.

Hunter made a face. "I know. I'm running behind. Did you get your Christmas shopping finished?"

"Malls are crazy right now. Yes, I think so. All but for you . . ." She shot him a smile, watching for his reaction.

He played back. "You mean because you have so many presents you need to buy me?"

She offered a playful punch. "You wish. How about you? Did you get the mics fixed?"

Hunter shook his head. "No. And the audio company can't make it before next Monday."

Denèe reacted. "What! That's not possible."

"Tell me about it." He swung around the circle drive and followed the street leading out of the subdivision. Once they got to Nuckols Road, his grandparents' house was just a few miles from the city.

She continued asking about the afternoon. "Everything else looking okay for dress rehearsal tonight?"

He nodded. "Pretty much. Still, I want to get there early, before everybody else."

"But we're staying for dinner, right?"

Hunter nodded. "Yes, hopefully quick. I'm thinking we get the Haskins introduced, grab a quick bite, then leave them to get acquainted while we head to church."

"That sounds good," said Denèe.

She turned up the volume on her cell phone and started Spotify to listen to music while they drove.

Turning into his grandparents' neighborhood, then approaching their house, Hunter could see that the Haskins weren't there yet. "Good, we beat them."

He pulled into the driveway, his VW Bug making its classic pinging sound from the exhaust as he parked and turned off the engine.

"I keep meaning to ask," she smiled while shaking her head, listening to the engine sputter then die, "what makes you want to drive this relic?"

"It's not a relic!" he said, huffy. "It's a classic. Besides, my dad drove it back when he was my age."

Denèe laughed. She loved teasing him. "That makes it a relic."

"I like that nobody else has one. Growing up, it was always parked in the back of Opa's garage, covered with a tarp. When I turned sixteen, Opa said I could have it. I spent that summer two years ago cleaning it up. I had to do some mechanical work." He patted the small dash proudly. "Now, here it is, like new."

Denèe couldn't help but laugh. "If you say so."

"Hey, there's no other car like it."

Denèe laughed. "True. The bug-eye lights remind me of my fourth-grade teacher, Mrs. Charleston. She was scary." She quit teasing. "Okay, I'll admit, your car is cute."

They climbed out and headed up the walk to the front door just as the Haskins's weathered SUV pulled into the drive and parked behind Hunter's VW.

Hunter and Denèe gave a wave.

The Haskins climbed out and gave a wave back. Everyone was dressed for the cold. The children, bundled up, hung close to their parents. The family walked up the drive toward Hunter and Denèe, who were waiting. Hunter could see that Karen Haskins was taking in his grandparents' large two-story home. It was impressive, he guessed, but to him, it was just his favorite place growing up because it was his grandparents'.

"We just came from the hospital," Karen apologized as they climbed the front brick steps. "We aren't very dressed up, I'm afraid."

"Then we match." Denèe laughed and pointed to her and Hunter's jeans and boots. "Who can get dressed up in this weather anyway? Except to stay warm."

"True." Karen smiled, looking more relaxed.

"Let's get out of this cold," Hunter said, ringing the doorbell.

Ellen was already opening the front door at the same time. "Come in, everybody."

They crowded into the foyer.

"Oma, these are the Haskins, who I've been telling you about."

"I'm Ellen Reid." She offered a warm smile. "Feel free to leave your boots and shoes at the door, if that's more comfortable. I know it's messy out there."

"I'm Karen and this is Al. It's so kind of you to invite us. Al and I are so grateful that Hunter and Denèe have befriended our son, Joey." Al offered an appreciative nod. "Joey can't stop talking about you two either."

"He's a special boy, Mr. Haskins," said Denèe. Hunter nodded.

"We've been hearing," said Ellen.

Karen put a hand on each of her children. "These are our youngest two, Maggie and Alex."

"Hi, kids," said Ellen, offering the children a big smile. "Hunter, help take everybody's coats and hang them in the hall closet if you would. Let's go into the living room and get acquainted while we wait for Hunter's grandfather, my husband, Max, to get here."

As they moved to the living room and got comfortable, Hunter was anxious to find out if there was any more news coming from the hospital. "Anything else happen after we left?"

Al Haskins now looked agitated. "Nobody at the hospital knows anything or saw anything. It makes no sense how a stranger can just walk in off the street, go up the elevator to the children's floor after visiting hours, walk past the nurse's station and down the hall past kids in their rooms, and no one know any the better."

Ellen, listening, shook her head. "That's what Hunter and Denèe were telling Max and me last night. It sounds so strange. What is the hospital doing about it?"

Karen answered, "Adding security at the hospital entrance and up on Joey's floor. Plus, checking on Joey frequently during the night."

She added, "Whoever this stranger is, Joey comes to life when he talks about his friend. Really, until this strange game showed up this morning," she looked over at Al, "we all thought this midnight visitor was just Joey's imagination."

Al nodded, his anger still showing. "I want to get to the bottom of who this person is. There is no way I'm going to accept a stranger visiting our son in the middle of the night."

Ellen nodded. "Totally understandable."

Hunter and Denèe listened. They already knew from earlier today that Al Haskins was a no-nonsense man.

Ellen added, "Hunter says that now a board game was found in Joey's room." She looked over at him. "Hunter, you didn't have time to get into much detail when you called earlier." She added, "I'm familiar with the game's name from the book and play."

Al studied Hunter and Denèe's reaction. They could tell he was still suspicious.

"That part makes no sense. It's a game nobody's heard of but in your church play. I'm not sure what to make of it."

"We don't know either," Hunter added hastily. "Oma, you know about the game. It dates to Roman times. Other than in the book, nobody has ever heard of it."

Denèe looked excited. "I told Hunter that this is like a *Nancy Drew* mystery."

"Yeah, except it's real," said Al.

Karen Haskins placed a hand on her husband's arm. "Whatever it means, I'm sure we'll find out. In the meantime, Joey is enjoying the game, which is harmless enough. It's just adding to the strangeness, with nobody offering us an answer as to how it got there."

"I hope you find out soon," Ellen answered.

Karen added, "On top of the game, the other strange thing is our son's talk about a miracle star due to appear. Again, something this stranger, who dresses in robes like a Middle Eastern sheik, has told him to look for."

"A miracle because of his donor backing out?" said Ellen.

The Haskins looked at each other and nodded. "It's true that Joey does need a miracle now," said Karen.

"Hunter and Denèe were telling Max and me. I'm so sorry. I know that must be devastating."

Al answered, "Totally. Joey was brought to the Children's Hospital last week to prepare for the procedure. As soon as we arrived, we heard the news. Now, the doctors say he's too weak to return home."

"Hunter and Denèe were saying that you are making the drive to the hospital every day and that your home is two hours away?"

They nodded.

"My husband, Max, is due any moment. I believe he has some news that can be of help."

As Ellen spoke, Max came into the room. "Did I just hear my name?" He grinned.

"Max, we didn't hear you come in," said Ellen.

"I just got here and heard you all talking." Max walked over to the Haskins, who had stood up to greet him.

"Max Reid."

"Nice to meet you, sir. I'm Al Haskins. This is my wife, Karen, and our two children, Maggie and Alex."

The two children looked up briefly from the video game that they had brought inside with them and smiled at Max.

"Glad you could come," said Max. "Hunter and his friend Denèe were sharing with us about your situation."

"Opa, I told the Haskins how you are wanting to help find them a place to stay near the hospital. So they don't have to make that drive every day."

Max nodded. "That's right, Hunter. And I've good news on that."

Before Max could continue, Ellen interrupted, "Max, why don't you share the news at dinner? Hunter and Denèe must leave soon for church. I want to make sure they eat first."

Ellen gave Denèe a wave to join her. "Denèe, if you could help me in the kitchen, please? Hunter, show the Haskins where they can wash up."

Ellen added, "I hope everyone likes Brunswick stew. Plus, I've baked homemade bread. With the weather, I thought something warm that sticks to the ribs might hit the spot."

"Sounds perfect." Karen and Al nodded.

A few minutes later, they were seated and getting acquainted while Ellen served up the stew. Quickly, the conversation turned to Joey and how his leukemia was out of remission. Now Joey needed a bone marrow transplant if he was to recover. Karen wiped away a tear.

Ellen replied, "We are so feeling for what Joey—your whole family is going through. Max, you said you have some helpful news?"

Max stopped eating. "Sure. I did a little checking around today. Don't know whether anyone mentioned, but I'm in the real estate business. My company has an apartment complex that we are refurbishing near the Children's Hospital. I was able to confirm that we have a two-bedroom unit available. It's furnished. It will allow you to come and go from the hospital, while having a place to sleep and fix meals."

Al looked at Max. "Thank you, but I don't know that we can afford—"

Max interrupted, "No rent is involved. Right now, it's vacant and available while we finish out the complex."

Karen buried her face in her husband's shoulder for a moment to hide her emotions.

Hunter and Denèe looked at each other, pleased.

Max continued, "This will let your family stay here, even if you need to go back to South Hill for your work, Al."

"I'm in between jobs at the moment," Al responded.

"That's what has made this so hard," said Karen.

"My company had some layoffs at the same time that we learned Joey's leukemia returned. It's been a double whammy."

"What kind of work do you do?" said Max.

"Anything to do with electronics. Recently, the company I worked for installed security and sound systems commercially."

Hunter and Denèe both perked up. "Sound systems?" Hunter repeated. He looked at Denèe. "Would that include fixing issues with lapel radio mics?"

"Sure. What's the problem?"

"It's for our church Christmas production. The mics our cast wears onstage just started acting up."

"The static is horrible, and their voices are breaking up," Denèe added, making a face.

"It's our church's audio system," Hunter explained. "It's a big sanctuary. To be heard, they have to wear mics."

"Could be a number of things. I would need to take a look in person."

"Would you?" Hunter asked, with Denèe nodding.

"Happy to. We must leave tonight to get back home before it's too late. How about I come by in the morning?" Al looked at Karen, who nodded. "Maybe give us till late morning. This travel is getting hard on the children."

Hunter let out a relieved sigh. "That would be radical. Tomorrow night is opening night, and our church's sound company can't make it until after Christmas."

"Thank you," gushed Denèe.

"Tomorrow, come ready to stay," said Max. "The unit is available."

"I can't tell you how much this means." Karen exchanged a look with her husband.

Al nodded appreciatively. "It's going to take a big weight off of us. Thank you again."

"If everyone is finished eating, let's do this," said Ellen. "Max, since the Haskins can't stay too long tonight, you all coordinate the accommodations while I bring in dessert."

She looked at her watch, then at Hunter and Denèe. "Aren't you two going to be late for rehearsal?"

Hunter checked his Apple watch. Time had gotten away, with all the conversation at the table. "We gotta go! I have your number, Mrs. Haskins ... Karen," he corrected himself. "I'll call you in the morning to coordinate."

They said quick goodbyes and grabbed their coats and headed for the door.

"I'll save you dessert," Ellen called after them. "Come by later if you can."

They were already out the door and running to Hunter's car.

Back in the dining room, Ellen was thoughtful. "Max, while we have dessert, I'd like to share with Karen and Al what we went through with our sick child once. With all the talk of a miracle for Joey, I'm thinking this might encourage you two," she spoke directly to the couple.

"We'd like that," said Karen.

"While I get dessert, Max, perhaps you can find a cartoon channel for the children, so they don't have to sit here with us adults. They can have dessert in the family room."

"Sure. Kids, come with me," Max said. "Show me what TV show you'd like to watch."

While Al went with Max to help get the kids settled, Karen followed Ellen into the kitchen.

With the two of them alone, Karen said, "Ellen, I'd really like to hear what happened with your family and your daughter. What happened that Christmas?"

Ellen looked at her guest. She could sense what the mother must be going through. "Max and I would love to share with you and Al. It was an extraordinary weekend."

Ellen noticed Karen's expression. Up until then, her face looked drawn with worry. For the first time, she looked relaxed.

"I can't wait to hear," Karen answered.

Chapter 9

Thursday, early evening, full-dress rehearsal
Westend Community Church

As soon as he pulled into the church parking lot, Hunter surveyed the vehicles there. Turnout looked normal. With the icy weather, he was concerned it might affect the members from making it to rehearsal. Tonight was critical. It was the only full-dress rehearsal before tomorrow night.

"Looks like people got here okay," Denèe observed.

He nodded, relieved. He had sent word out earlier that if anyone was concerned about driving in this weather, to call and someone would pick them up. No one had called, so he had to assume everyone was there.

He checked his Apple watch. It said 6:30. "Hopefully, everyone got here by 5:30 for any last-minute costume issues."

Denèe patted his arm. "No worries there. You know Miss Cho will be sure that everyone is fitted perfectly."

Denée's voice got excited. "I can't wait to see everyone in full costume. Things are finally feeling real."

Hunter knew from earlier productions that by the time full-dress rehearsal arrived, reality always set in. It was an adrenaline rush, knowing the show was about to go live.

"Did you get a chance to chat with Wayne about the mics? Maybe he's fixed the problem by now."

Hunter shook his head. "Not yet. Hopefully, he and I can figure it out tonight. But can you believe that Al Haskins knows commercial sound systems? What are the odds of that? Just when we need an expert."

Denèe looked thoughtful. "All these coincidences happening since we met Joey yesterday. It's feels like we're missing something."

He knew how intuitive she was. "What do you think is going on?"

She studied him now. "I don't know. But the game showing up in Joey's room really has changed everything."

Hunter had to agree. "Yeah, that can't just be by coincidence. So, what does it mean?"

"I think Joey's mysterious visitor is the key. If we can discover who he is—now that everyone knows he's real—that will explain what's going on."

Hunter was trying to follow Denèe's train of thought. "I agree. He's not just some ordinary stranger off the street. Not dressed the way that Joey describes, and showing up after visiting hours. Meanwhile, cameras don't show any sign of him being there. Plus, don't forget that he's a stargazer who's come to help Joey discover a miracle star."

Denèe gave a shiver. "This whole thing gives me the chills. And not from your cold car!"

Hunter grinned. "You would add that."

She smiled back. "I'm kidding. We need a little levity."

Denèe leaned down to gaze through the windshield and up at the night sky. "It's connected to the book, *The Legend*, Hunter. I feel certain of that."

"What are you thinking we should do?"

She reached over and took his hand. "I think we let this all play out. At some point, we'll know what's going on."

"I agree."

She gave his hand a squeeze. "We better get inside. By now, everyone is wondering where we are."

Climbing out of the car, they grabbed hands for balance to make their way across the icy parking lot to the fellowship hall entrance. It was where everyone would be mingling, waiting to start rehearsal.

Stepping inside, they stomped their feet to kick off the ice. The fellowship hall was a large room capable of holding a few hundred members for a social.

Hunter scanned the room. A group was gathered around the coffee bar, already dressed up.

Everyone noticed them come in.

Somebody called out from across the room, "Glad you two could join us tonight!"

Hunter grinned and kidded back, "We are too!"

Just then, Miss Cho entered the hall from the door that led to the costume fitting room. Seeing the two of them, she headed their way.

Offering Hunter her familiar frown, Miss Cho challenged, "You're late, Mr. Director."

Hunter mumbled to Denèe, "You'd think I showed up late all the time."

"I heard that," the elderly Korean woman quipped.

Hunter countered, "Miss Costume Designer, I came late to stay out of your way during costume fitting."

Denèe shook her head, listening to their banter.

Miss Cho grunted. "You're in my way now, Mr. Director." Turning to Denèe, her frown now a friendly smile. "Why do you stay with this boy? You're too pretty for him."

Denèe laughed. "Somebody has to make sure our play is a success, Miss Cho. How are things going tonight? Are the costumes fitting okay?"

"Not good, but Miss Cho will fix it!" She turned to head to the coffee bar. "I'll go get my tea, then I'll be back to the dressing room. Nobody knows how to wear their costume!"

She offered one last frown. "Mr. Director, you need to get to work. People are waiting!"

Denèe chuckled, watching the Korean seamstress shuffle off. "I think she likes you, Hunter."

Hunter scowled. "Whatever makes you think that?"

"Anyone can tell that you two enjoy each other." She added, "I'll bet she's already fixed a dozen costume issues."

Hunter had to agree. "Miss Cho is good at her job. I'll say that."

Josh Whitaker, who was mingling over at the coffee bar, now headed their way. He was already dressed as Micah the shepherd boy. Hunter had to admit that he looked the part. Especially with the youthful beard he had grown out just for the role. Now, if he could finally get his lines right!

"Hey guys!" he said, approaching.

Denèe whistled. "Josh, you look great! Doesn't he, Hunter?"

"Like a real shepherd. How are those lines coming, Josh?"

The high school senior winced. "Sorry about last night. I had a lot going on before coming to practice. Applying for college stuff. No worries. I'll be ready tonight."

His expression suddenly brightened. "Did you hear the news?"

They both gave him a questioning look. "What news?" asked Hunter.

"Caelum's been talking about an astrological event that astronomers are calling the reappearance of the Bethlehem Star."

Hunter and Denèe exchanged a look.

Denèe answered, "We saw the news about that. What is Caelum saying?"

"Something about a Great Conjunction. Planets coming together to form a giant star. Pretty cool, huh? Right in time for this weekend and our play."

Denèe and Hunter exchanged a knowing look. Somehow, they weren't surprised that Caelum would know about the event.

Hunter gazed over at the coffee bar. "Where is he now?"

Josh shrugged. "Probably in the dressing room. You should have him share about the event with the cast. It will get everyone excited!"

Denèe nudged Hunter. "We can get more details from Caelum later. Right now, you should find Wayne. Meanwhile, what can I do?"

"Gather everybody up onstage. Mr. Wilson mentioned today that he wants to give a little pep talk for tomorrow night."

Hunter headed for the sanctuary to find Wayne. Over his shoulder, he admonished Josh, "Make sure you've got your lines down tonight!"

Josh called back, "No worries. I'm Micah tonight!"

Fifteen minutes later, Denèe had everyone gathered on the raised stage. Thirty strong, between cast and set crew, they had formed a semicircle around Hunter to listen.

Hunter studied the group, admiring the costumes. "You guys look great." It was true. The costumes really were eye-catching. They had better be. Mr. Wilson had spent a small fortune to make sure every part of the production was theater-level quality.

Hunter began, "Before Mr. Wilson joins us to say a word, Denèe and I want to share some very strange happenings. We're thinking they might somehow be connected to the play."

He gave a wave for her to come stand beside him.

"Denèe, why don't you start by telling everyone what's been happening?"

She walked over, stood beside Hunter, and acknowledged a few in the group. "Some of you were with us yesterday visiting the kids at the Children's Hospital. While there, Hunter and I met a special boy named Joey Haskins. Joey is in critical need of a bone marrow transplant, after his leukemia relapsed. No doubt, you met some special kids too."

Nods.

"You'll find what I'm about to share strangely mysterious. Like what Hunter and I are feeling. It started about a week ago, when Joey returned to the Children's Hospital to prepare for the procedure. But when he arrived, he and his parents learned that the donor had backed out."

Groans rippled through the group.

Denèe acknowledged them. "I know. What he needs now is a miracle, with his condition worsening." She glanced at Hunter, pausing to let him comment.

Hunter frowned. "Sadly, yes. Here's the reason why we're sharing. Joey started telling us about a stranger who visits him late at night, after visiting hours. The man he described dresses in robes and a turban, like those worn in the Middle East. Joey started telling us how this midnight stranger was there to help him discover a miracle star. It all sounded like the vivid imagination of a boy who's watched such things in cartoons."

Knowing smiles came from parents in the group.

Denèe jumped in, "That's what we thought—at first. "

Hunter added, "When we met his mother, she said the same. That her son had created the fantasy to deal with his crisis."

Denèe added, "Karen Haskins, his mother, went on to tell us how no one else had seen this stranger come or go. Not the nurse's station or security. Much less, someone dressed like Joey described."

"And coming at midnight," Hunter added. "That was yesterday. Then this morning, that all changed."

The group was listening intently now.

"Tell everybody what happened, Denèe."

She nodded. "So I had called Joey's mother this morning to invite her family for dinner at Hunter's grandparents'. Last night, after practice, we went by their house. Hunter wanted to tell them about the family, their crisis, and that they had no place to stay in Richmond. Every day, they've been visiting their son, making a four-hour round-trip drive with two small children. Hunter's grandparents, Max and Ellen Reid, they attend church here, for any of you who don't know them. The Reid's offered to invite them to dinner to get acquainted and to offer the family help."

Hunter nodded for Denèe to continue.

"So that's why I called Mrs. Haskins. When she answered, she sounded hysterical. Turns out, this stranger that Joey's been saying visits him is real."

There were sounds of surprise. Everyone was curious now.

"How did they find that out?" someone asked.

"This is the strangest part of all." Denèe turned to Hunter. "You tell them."

Hunter walked over to a nearby prop, a faux boulder. Resting atop the boulder was a reproduction model of the board game, Game of Mercenaries. He picked up the leather playing board. "You all know this game and the role it plays in the escape scene."

They nodded.

"Well, this was the game they found in Joey's room this morning."

Chet, one of the set crew, spoke up, "Hunter, I'm having trouble following you. Are you saying *this* game was in this boy's room?"

Hunter looked at the prop serving as the game board. "Not this one, of course, but the same game."

Denèe added, "When we heard that Joey was calling it Game of Mercenaries, we headed straight down to the hospital this morning to see. "

"That can't be just a coincidence," Bob, who managed the stage crew, commented. The group nodded their agreement.

Denèe continued, "That's what Hunter and I think too. Here's the other thing. When we went to see, we were shocked. The game in his room is ancient. Honestly, it looks like it could be a relic dating back to the Roman Empire."

"You're talking 2,000 years ago," someone added, skeptical.

"Exactly," said Hunter.

The room was quiet while everyone tried to digest what they had just heard. Finally, Sheila Mae, the school drama teacher and play narrator, spoke, "So, what is it you two think is happening?"

Hunter and Denèe exchanged a shrug.

Denèe answered, "That's just it, Sheila Mae, we can't figure out what is going on."

Hunter explained, "The reason we are sharing all this is that everything seems eerily connected to our play."

Shelia Mae continued, "You're saying this obsolete game somehow just showed up?" She added, "Brought by someone looking like a sheik that nobody else sees?"

Hunter nodded. "That about says it."

Denèe continued what she was saying, "So, when we got there this morning, the hospital staff was in a tizzy. Here was this stranger visiting a child, and nobody was the wiser. Adding to that, the security cameras positioned in the halls and all floors showed no one coming or going during the night. Much less someone dressed in Middle Eastern robes."

Hunter added, "They are telling us, starting tonight, that security will post a guard at the entrance to the floor. In the meantime, Joey's parents are threatening legal action against the hospital. Obviously concerned for the safety of their son."

"I'd sue too," said a cast member. There were nods of agreement.

"What does the boy say about all this?" Sheila Mae asked.

"Just that he tried to tell the adults about his midnight visitor, but no one would believe him. To your question, Sheila Mae, Joey seems oblivious to all the hoopla."

Hunter smiled. "He's too busy having fun playing his new game with whoever will join him."

"What about this miracle star he's searching for?" they asked.

Denèe explained, "Yesterday, as soon as we met Joey, he wanted to make a gold foil star to hang in his room window, to remind him to be looking for a miracle star. His midnight visitor has told him that if he sees this special star in the sky and discovers its secret meaning, he can find his miracle."

"Meaning a bone marrow transplant donor," Hunter added.

Now Hunter searched the group. He was thinking now of what Josh had said about what Caelum was talking about. "Anyone seen Caelum?"

"I'm here." A voice came from behind the group. Caelum was just joining the meeting.

"Caelum, tell everyone what you were saying earlier about a rare astronomical event."

Caelum walked to the front of the group. He was in costume to play the Magi's servant. "I was sharing about a planetary conjunction set to occur over Christmas. An extremely rare event when Jupiter and Saturn converge to create the illusion of a brilliant star. What many are calling the Bethlehem Star."

Listening to Caelum, Hunter couldn't help but think how fortunate they were that Caelum had come along to fill the role.

"You've heard me talk about the Magi, how they were Zoroastrian astrologers. Known as stargazers back then. It's believed this event is what told them a messiah was born."

Hunter saw how the group was listening. Everyone considered him to be the expert on the Magi.

Caelum turned to Hunter and Denèe. "Perhaps this is the event the boy's midnight friend is calling a miracle star?"

Someone asked if Joey was well enough to attend the play.

"He wants to," Denèe answered. "But right now, his doctor says he's too vulnerable to go out in the cold."

"Can our church do anything to support Joey and his family?" someone asked.

A voice in the back spoke up, "Hunter, if I may answer that?"

It was Mr. Wilson joining them.

"Of course," Hunter answered.

The arts and music minister walked to the front of the group.

"Hunter," he began, "you maybe haven't heard that your grandparents, Max and Ellen Reid, for those who don't know, called the church today. The staff is looking into what we can do to support the Haskins. I heard they came for dinner at your grandparents this evening."

"Denèe and I were there to make the introductions."

"That's why we were late!" Denèe had to add.

"Good news too," Hunter added, "Joey's dad, Al Haskins, will be helping to find out what the issue is with our mics."

Claps.

"Excellent," Mr. Wilson said, turning to gaze across the empty auditorium. "Tomorrow night, our sanctuary will be filled to capacity for each show. As you know, Hunter has turned an amazing story into an inspiring play. Hats off to that achievement. Now it's up to all of you to give a performance that people will remember long after they leave. I know you will!"

He paused, then, "One more thing. Following rehearsal, there will be pizza in the fellowship hall."

The group clapped, excited about that treat.

He gave Hunter a nod.

Hunter took the cue. "Okay, let's clear the stage to get ready for the first act. We have a real performance to make happen tonight!"

Chapter 10

Thursday night, 8:00 p.m.
Children's Hospital

Dr. Elizabeth Stern was about to end her shift. Dr. Ellie, what her young patients liked to call her, wanted to check on Joey one more time. She had checked on him a couple of times during her shift. Especially now as his condition was starting to take its toll.

After all the hullabaloo following the discovery of the game in his room, she wanted to see how he was faring. She shook her head, amazed, thinking about it. From the first night he arrived until this morning, no one believed him about his midnight friend. Now the atmosphere on the floor was changed. Everyone was feeling the pressure from corporate to find out who this person was and how they got onto the floor unobserved.

She reached Joey's partially closed door and peeked inside. The room was quiet. No TV on. Joey lay there staring at the window.

She followed his gaze. His eyes were focused on the gold star dangling in front of the window, slowly turning from the air vent, reflecting flashes of light. He turned his head just briefly enough to see her walk in, then returned his gaze to the window. Her young patient was clearly depressed.

She came over to his bedside to check his vital signs on the monitor. Her face registered concern at the readings.

"How are you feeling?"

"Not good."

She knew that already. His skin was pale. She felt his forehead. It was cool, clammy even, indicating his low red blood cell count was causing anemia. Attaching her stethoscope, she listened to his chest. His breathing was more labored than before. The monitor showed a pulse of over 155. Normal for his age was between 75 and 118. His body was fighting for oxygen.

"My bones hurt," he said, looking her in the eyes, his expression vulnerable.

She nodded that she understood. It was as if she could feel his pain. As a resident oncologist, she had seen enough children in Joey's situation. She made a mental note to increase the pain medication in his drip IV.

"Joey, I'm going to give you something to help you sleep."

Joey shook his head. "I don't want to go to sleep, Dr. Ellie. My friend Shaz is coming to see me."

She looked over at the ancient board game resting on the tray table. When she heard the name earlier today, she had looked it up. Game of Mercenaries, or Ludus latrunculorum, its Latin name, sounded familiar. Sure enough, she had seen the game while visiting one of the museums in Jerusalem during her college days. As a history buff, she found her Jewish ancestry fascinating. Especially back when Rome had occupied Palestine.

"Will you be playing your game with your friend tonight?"

He frowned. "I don't think I feel like it. Shaz promised me that he's bringing his chart to show me how to discover the miracle star."

This really was too fascinating. The idea of a stranger visiting Joey while the hospital was on full alert. She wondered what the report might say come morning.

"It would be nice to meet your friend." Dr. Ellie smiled.

"I already asked him. He doesn't want to meet anyone else."

"So, when this star appears, what happens then?"

"Shaz says when I see the star, I must discover its secret message to receive my miracle."

Joey let out an exasperated breath and pointed at the window. "Dr. Ellie, I don't know what to do. I can't see the stars from in here."

She was already thinking about that. If Joey believed seeing a star would bring his miracle, how could she not help make that happen? She had already decided to tell him about the hospital's outdoor park.

"Joey, our hospital has a kid's park on the rooftop that's open to the sky. Do you think it would help if you went up there to look?"

Joey's eyes lit up. "Yes! Can I go?"

She offered a smile. "I'm going to talk to my boss, the floor's head doctor. Let me see what I can arrange. Don't get your hopes up quite yet."

Joey returned a steady gaze. "I know you can get it approved, Dr. Ellie."

Now that she said that, she knew she could not let him down. She gave an encouraging pat. "Just keep your spirits up, okay?"

When a child got to Joey's stage, the will to live played a huge role in the fight.

He offered her his first big smile since she walked in.

"I'll check back first thing in the morning when I start my shift. Keep your fingers crossed." She gave him an affectionate squeeze.

As she left, she felt her own spirit's lift. Her hope now was that this mysterious stranger friend was not building him up for disappointment. Star or no star, she knew Joey had to receive his bone marrow transplant soon!

11:00 p.m.

Outside in the hallway leading into the Critical Care Ward, a uniformed security guard stood and stretched. It was time for Snoot—what everyone called him—to make another security walk. Tonight's shift was putting him to sleep. At least now, he could stretch his legs and keep himself awake by walking around.

Snoot knew a little of why he was guarding the entrance tonight. But really? He was supposed to be on the lookout for some guy dressed like a Middle Eastern sheik! That was how the hospital's chief of security, Snoot's boss, had described the guy. Snoot's job was simple. Stop anyone not authorized from entering the ward.

He gave his legs a shake so his pants hung straight and adjusted his uniform and belt. Then he took out his key card and swiped the entry lock. The system clicked, unlocking the double doors. Stepping inside the ward, he looked around to make a quick assessment. Twenty feet away was the nurse's station. A lone nurse sat there studying her computer screen. The nurse's name was Erica. He had briefly met her during his last round.

"Still here?" she asked, looking up.

"Yeah. I've got an all-nighter. How about you?"

"Same. Night shift runs till six in the morning. You are here about the Haskins boy, right?"

He nodded. "You think someone's been sneaking in here late at night?" Snoot asked.

"Honestly, I don't see how. From what I'm told, nothing shows on the hall cameras. There must be some other logical explanation."

"Yeah. Well, I can tell you, whoever this person is, he's not coming through me to get on the floor."

"Me either," she agreed.

Snoot headed to the Haskins boy's room. He paused before slowly opening the door and secretly peeked inside. The boy lay there. The room was quiet. The boy turned and briefly looked at Snoot, then returned his gaze to the window. Snoot quickly scanned the room.

"He's not here," the Haskins boy said.

"Okay. I'm required to check anyway. You alright?"

The boy nodded. Snoot looked at the game on the tray table. All this ruckus over that game. Shaking his head, he offered, "Call the nurse if you need anything." He didn't need to say that, but at least it was something to say.

Closing the door, Snoot continued his walk down the hall. He would cover both directions before returning to his post.

Finally finished, he went back to the hallway. He took out his two-way radio to report. "This is Snoot. I just finished checking the floor, along with the boy's room. All quiet. Nobody in there."

The voice on the other end was the chief. He was staying after normal hours to manage the crisis. "You're sure?"

"Quiet, just like a morgue, chief."

"I told you, don't use that word. Okay, call me if you see anyone who's not part of the hospital."

"Will do, chief."

Confident that no one was gonna get past him, Snoot settled into his chair and picked up the gossip magazine. It was the one he grabbed from the visitor waiting room on his way up. At least the gossip magazine filled his time. Before he went on his round, he had started reading about how the rich and famous celebrated Christmas—jets, island hopping, and parties. Some people had all the luck in life. He yawned. His yawn this time was long and harder than earlier. He closed his eyes. For just a moment, he promised himself. In less than a minute, Snoot was snoring.

Midnight

A tall, bearded man of Middle Eastern appearance, wearing the customary white medical coat of a physician, walked down the main corridor leading to the oncology floor entrance.

Just ahead, a security guard sat blocking the double doors. His head had fallen back against the wall behind him. He was fast asleep, evidenced by his snoring. Shaz smiled as he quietly stepped past the guard. Then, using the guard's own keycard resting on the table, he entered through the double doors. Passing by the nurse's station, presently unattended, he continued down the hall to his young friend's room.

Cracking open the door, he peered inside. Joey was waiting.

Seeing his friend, Joey came to life. "Shaz! I knew you'd come! What are you doing dressed like a doctor?"

Shaz let out a deep-throated laugh. "They are looking for a man in robes. So, I changed what to wear tonight."

Joey laughed. "I wondered how you would get past the security guards. One has been checking in on me every hour."

Shaz smiled. "I know. They aren't looking for a doctor on their surveillance cameras."

"Did you bring your charts?" Joey pushed the button to raise his bed to a sitting position. He looked excited.

"Of course, like I promised." Shaz tapped the satchel hanging at his side.

Coming bedside, Shaz pulled out a chart and spread it open across the bed.

For a minute, Joey studied the ancient chart. It showed circles of differing sizes, with lines connecting them. "What does it mean?"

Shaz smiled. "What you are seeing, young Joey, is how the heavens looked 2,000 years ago."

"Where is the miracle star?"

Shaz pointed. "See these two circles? They are shown moving together. When they do, it will create one huge star."

Joey's eyes grew large. "So that's what I'm looking for? Two stars coming together?"

"Actually, it is two planets converging that gives the appearance of one giant star."

"Will it be easy for me to find it with all the other stars up there?"

Shaz nodded. "You can't miss it. When the miracle star appears, it will be much larger and brighter than anything else in the sky."

Joey looked at the chart again. "I don't understand where the miracle part comes in?"

"Good question. The miracle is what happened when this special star appeared 2,000 years ago."

Joey studied his friend. "What happened?"

Shaz answered, "That is the mystery. You must discover the answer for yourself. When you do discover it, you will find your miracle."

"What if I can't discover the answer? What happens then?"

Shaz gave a deep-throated laugh. "Do not worry, my young friend. For now, set your attention on searching for this special star to appear. When you see it, you will understand its mystery."

Joey couldn't hold back his news any longer. "Guess what, Shaz? My doctor—Dr. Ellie—told me earlier tonight how the hospital has a children's park up on the roof. She's going to ask permission for me to go up there. That way, I can see the open sky and find the miracle star."

Legend of the Wooden Star

"That is excellent!"

"When should I go up there? What night?"

Shaz studied the chart again, then thought a moment. "By my calculation, the miracle star will be at its brightest from tomorrow night through the weekend."

Joey's face lit up. "So, I need to go up there soon!"

Shaz nodded. "I can see your doctor friend wants to help you. That is excellent."

Looking peaceful now, Joey laid his head back against his pillow.

Shaz gave Joey a gentle squeeze. "I need to leave you to rest. We will talk later."

Exhausted, Joey didn't resist. Instead, he closed his eyes. Immediately, he was asleep.

Shaz lowered the bed to the prone position. As he studied his young friend, he could see that Joey's condition was dire.

He spoke in a low voice, "Now, young Joey, it is time for me to put into motion what needs to happen for your miracle."

Slipping out of the room, he retraced his steps to exit the hospital. Security was looking for a man dressed in Middle Eastern robes, not a doctor making rounds. Shaz allowed himself a smile. Of course, it didn't hurt either that the cameras were temporarily off.

Chapter 11

Friday morning
Downtown Richmond,
near the Children's Hospital

It was nine o'clock when Al and Karen, along with their two younger children, arrived at the prearranged address to meet Max. Climbing out their SUV, they headed to the apartment building, where Max was already waiting outside.

He waved them over. "Good morning. How was the trip in?"

Karen looked at Al and sighed. "It's been getting longer each day, Max."

Max offered an understanding nod. "It's why you need this place to stay. It will allow you to settle in close to your son." Max pointed across Broad Street to the Children's Hospital a few blocks away. "He's just a short walk."

"We can't thank you enough," Al said, with Karen nodding and all smiles.

"Come on, let's go take a look." Max led them inside to the elevator to the four-story apartment building.

"Like I said when we talked last night, the unit is fully furnished. Furnished units are what the students at the nearby university look for, and why we do it."

Fifteen minutes later, they had finished touring the two-bedroom, two-bath unit.

"It's perfect, Max. We can't thank you enough," a relieved Karen said, offering Max a hug.

"Glad to help," said Max. "Call me if you need anything."

After Max left, Karen walked out onto the balcony that overlooked Broad Street. In the distance a half mile away, the Children's Hospital was visible. Looking at Al, who had followed her, she wiped a tear. "I can't believe this is happening, Al. I'm so relieved."

He gave her a hug. "Me too. I'll get our bags out of the SUV so you and the kids can settle while I go to meet up with Hunter. See if I can fix his microphone issue."

Climbing back into the family's SUV, Al inputed the church address Hunter gave him into Google maps. Maps showed it was twenty-five minutes away. With that, he pulled off and headed to the west side of the city's suburbs.

Legend of the Wooden Star

Westend Community Church

Denèe met Al as he came in the church side entrance, like they arranged ahead of time.

"Good morning, Mr. Haskins."

"Good morning, Denèe, and please call me Al."

"Sorry." She starter over, "Al, Hunter had to run over to the administration building. He asked me to show you to the sound booth. It's located on the balcony."

On the way up the stairs, Denèe asked, "Did you and Karen meet Hunter's grandfather this morning?"

"We did. Max Reid is an amazing man."

"I take it everything turned out ok. Will you be staying in town now?"

"Yes, the apartment is perfect. Totally furnished. Plus, only a few blocks from the hospital. Such generous people, Max and Ellen are."

"I just met them the other night. I agree. Very special people."

They reached the top level. The balcony, which curved around the back of the auditorium, added another one-third to the seating capacity of a thousand down below. Centered in the back was a glassed-in cubicle that housed the console that controlled the church's audio system. Next to it were cameras on either side for filming services. From its elevated position, it offered a clear view of the stage area at the front of the auditorium. The facility was impressive, with an orchestra pit just below the stage.

Wayne was already there in the booth. Hunter had asked him to come in to meet with Al.

Denèe made the introductions. "Wayne, this is Al Haskins, the gentlemen Hunter told you about. Al's here to help fix the microphone issue."

Wayne waved for Al to join him in the sound booth. "Take a look around. I'm hoping it's not too big of an issue to fix. Tonight, the play opens. Problem is, we can't get the company who services the system out here before then."

"When did the mics start to act up?" Al asked, surveying the mixer console.

"Everything was working fine till the other night."

Al nodded and listened while he assessed the sound equipment. "Your church has a Cadillac model. No expense spared here."

Wayne agreed. "Yeah, the facility was built for professional performances like the Christmas play. We offer major productions at Christmas and Easter, open to the entire community."

Al nodded. "Nice. Usually, when there's a problem with wireless mics, it's an antenna issue. Has the antenna been moved by chance?"

"Not that I know of."

Al looked at the control console. "How many wireless microphones are being used at one time?"

Wayne thought. "About a dozen last count."

"That is a lot. Had you added any just prior to the issue?"

"Come to think of it, yes." Wayne looked over at Denèe, who was standing nearby listening. "Denèe, we added two more mics on stage the other night for the shepherds, right?"

"We sure did."

Al nodded. "Okay, now we're getting somewhere. First, I want to look over the main console here. Then let's look at where the antennas are mounted."

Denèe interrupted, "If you two don't need me here, Hunter has a dozen things for me to get done."

"We're good," said Al. "Tell Hunter we'll figure this out."

"He'll be relieved to hear that." She smiled. "One thing to check off the list!"

Denèe left to go meet Hunter. It would be nonstop the rest of the day, she knew, until the curtains opened tonight.

Noon

Hunter and Denèe were on the stage talking with the set crew about how to stabilize the palm tree prop, which was still threatening to topple.

Denèe gave instructions. "Guys, let's attach two more guy wires to make sure the heavy prop doesn't topple over in the middle of the show."

Just then, Hunter's cell chirped. It was his grandmother. He walked away to answer. "Hey, Oma, what's up?"

"How are things going?"

Hunter made a face. "Crazy, Oma!"

"I won't keep you. You heard that your grandfather met with the Haskins and got them situated in the apartment?"

"I did hear. In fact, Al was here earlier fixing our mic issue."

"Isn't it amazing that sound systems happen to be Al's specialty?"

"That's what Denèe and I were saying."

Ellen continued, "The reason I'm calling is that I just got off the phone with Karen Haskins. I've offered to keep Joey company tonight at the hospital. It will let Karen bring her two younger children to attend the play."

"That's really nice of you, Oma."

"Here's the thing, I need the *Legend* book back from Denèe. I want to read the story to Joey. It will help him not feel left out. Is Denée there where I can speak with her?"

Hunter checked to see. "She's right here. Hang on."

Hunter waved at Denèe, who was still talking with the set crew. "Oma is on the phone. She'd like to speak to you."

Denèe's face brightened. She took the phone. "Hi, Oma."

"Denèe. I know you and Hunter are busy, so I won't keep you. I was telling Hunter that I talked with Karen Haskins a few minutes ago. I've offered to stay with Joey tonight so she and Al can take the younger children to see the play."

"That's very thoughtful of you, Oma."

"The reason I'm calling is that I'd like to read *Legend* to Joey. I know we just lent it to you, but I really don't want him to feel left out."

"Actually, I brought it with me. It's in my car. How can I get it to you, Oma?"

"If you're going to be there, I'll stop by."

Denèe chuckled. "Believe me, Hunter's not going to let me go anywhere else!"

She finished the call and handed the phone back to Hunter. "Your Oma is stopping by shortly. Shall we put her to work?"

Hunter laughed. "That's an idea. Hey, did you get the palm tree issue fixed?"

She nodded. "You said Al got the mic issue fixed?"

"He did. He's going to help run the sound booth. Mr. Wilson has agreed that the church will pay him. That should help their family."

Denèe shook her head in wonder. "A sound man coming along just when we needed him. Another amazing coincidence."

Hunter couldn't disagree.

Chapter 12

Friday evening, 5:00 p.m.
Children's Hospital

Ellen Reid checked in at the welcome desk down in the lobby, got directions, and headed up to Joey's room, where she and Karen had arranged to meet.

She knocked on Joey's door.

"Come in." It was Karen Haskins's voice.

Seeing it was Ellen, Karen walked over to meet her. The women embraced.

"Ellen, I want you to meet my son, Joey. Joey, this is Mrs. Reid, Hunter's grandmother."

Joey offered a faint smile and weakly said hi.

Ellen came close to Joey. "It's very nice to meet you, Joey. I've heard you've been having quite the adventure since you got here."

Joey shrugged. "I wish I were back home and not here."

That struck a chord with Ellen. "I heard about your donor backing out, and now you are in search of your miracle. I'd like to hear about your visitor friend and this miracle star. Would you like to share?"

Joey offered a weak smile. "Okay."

"Then we'll begin reading *Legend of the Wooden Star*. It's what Hunter used to write the play."

Joey's eyes lit up. "You brought it?"

"I did."

"Can I see it?" He pushed the control button to raise the top half of his bed to a sitting position.

Ellen handed Joey the book to examine. The leather cover was worn from age, the book's title faded.

"It looks really old."

"It is. We don't know who wrote it. The author is anonymous. I think you'll find it to be a fascinating story." She smiled. "And it involves a miracle star."

That got Joey's attention. "Like what I'm looking for!"

Ellen nodded. "That's what I hear."

Karen looked pleased, watching them get acquainted.

She gathered up her things. "I better go. Al and the children are waiting for me at the apartment. Thank you and Max for everything."

Ellen reached over, took Karen's hand, and gave it a squeeze. "We are happy that we can help. Anything for this wonderful boy of yours."

Joey, listening, smiled.

Karen walked over and gave her son a kiss on the forehead. "Have fun with Mrs. Reid. When your dad and I get back from the play, we'll come back to see you."

Karen slipped out while Ellen pulled a chair up close to Joey. "Before I read the story, I want to hear about this mysterious friend of yours that no one else sees." She looked over at the game. "And I want to hear all about this game he brought you. Which, by the way, is in the story we will read together."

"What do you want to know?"

"Anything you want to tell me. I'm excited to hear."

Westend Community Church

Two hours before curtains

Hunter checked his watch for the umpteenth time. Curtain time was fast approaching. As he walked around checking on the cast and crew, he could feel everyone's nervous energy. Nobody was just walking anymore. Instead, there was a kind of frantic hurrying.

With less than two hours before the doors opened and ushers starting to seat people, there was still so much to do. He shook his head. So much, you'd think they hadn't been preparing hard the past couple of weeks!

He knew from past experiences being in plays, that there was never a shortage of details to check on during final countdown to curtain time. The key was to make sure no real crisis suddenly sabotaged the performance enough for the audience to notice. There were always small crises that were going to pop up. It was the last-minute crises that made a director nervous. So long as the audience didn't pick-up on it and distract from the performance, that was most important. The cast and crew could enjoy a laugh about the minor screw-ups later.

He had just come from backstage, where Denèe was busy helping Miss Cho get the cast dressed out. One thing that helped was that everybody had tried on their costumes, and any issues were already resolved. That's why the full-dress rehearsal was so important. When the cast came in, the focus would be on makeup, wigs, beards, and the ladies' hair in keeping with ancient times.

In the meantime, Hunter went back to the auditorium for a last look around. He checked the visibility of the props to make sure the audience seated in the side aisles could see everything.

A booming sound startled him. Then the words, "Testing, testing, testing." He looked up and saw Wayne in the sound booth. Al wasn't due until a half-hour before curtains. Hunter knew it was because he was bringing Karen and the kids.

"Everything good?" he yelled up at Wayne.

Wayne answered over the sound system, "Thanks to Al."

Hunter smiled. Over the speakers, Wayne's voice sounded like the voice of God.

A hand tapped Hunter's shoulder. He turned to see who it was. It was Mr. Wilson.

"Feeling the jitters?" He smiled.

Hunter drew in a breath and exhaled hard. "I'm thinking about how so many things could go wrong."

Mr. Wilson chuckled. "That's normal. In fact, it's the sign of a good director." Mr. Wilson put a reassuring hand on Hunter's shoulder. "I've been there. Right now, I'm guessing your brain is going 90 miles an hour."

Hunter blew hard. "At least!"

Before walking away, Mr. Wilson offered the traditional good luck used in theater. "Break a leg."

It was a weird phrase that sounded like a curse, but Hunter had learned in drama class that it meant the opposite. During Elizabethan times, when theater was the main source of entertainment, instead of clapping, the audience would stomp their feet to applaud. If they really enjoyed a show, they would bang their chairs on the floor. Sometimes, so enthusiastically, a chair leg would break. Thus, the expression.

Right then, one of the set crew, Bryce, was headed Hunter's way. Judging by his expression, whatever it was wasn't good.

"I think here's your crisis," Mr. Wilson said and hurried off.

Bryce came up out of breath. "You heard Tom was running late with Penelope?"

"Yes . . ."

"We found out why. On the way to bring Penelope, his trailer got a flat tire. Right now, he's stuck on the side of the road."

Hunter felt like he got the breath knocked out of him. "You gotta be kidding."

"Wish I was." Bryce scowled.

"What are we doing to help?"

"Two from our team have gone to find Tom. I'm waiting to hear a status. But I wanted you to know."

Hunter's first thought was the camel. "Is Penelope okay?"

Legend of the Wooden Star

"We asked. Tom said she's fine."

Hunter nodded, relieved. "Okay, keep me updated."

Hunter watched Bryce scurry off.

This was that last-minute emergency that he had feared would happen. He looked up and said a prayer, "Lord, don't let there be another one!"

Chapter 13

Children's Hospital

For the first hour, Joey had shared about his friend Shaz's visits and how he had come to help Joey find his miracle.

Now he asked, "Oma, do you want to play my new game?"

By now, Ellen had Joey calling her by the name her grandchildren called her.

Ellen nodded. "First, you have to show me how."

"It's not hard. Can you slide the tray table over my bed?"

Ellen positioned the table over Joey so he could easily move the piece. Now she studied the leather board and stone pieces. It really did look ancient.

Joey started explaining, "The board is called the 'city.' Pretend you're fighting a battle and trying to kill all your opponent's soldiers."

Ellen nodded, keeping her face serious. "Okay."

He handed her the bag of stones, then emptied his bag on the tray table behind his side of the board. Ellen did the same.

"We each have fifteen stones—yours are light-colored—mine are dark. Shaz says the pieces are called 'dogs.'"

Ellen laughed. "Really, *dogs*?"

Joey laughed. "All the names are weird. Like this big stone." He held his up. You have one too. These are called the 'dux.' Shaz says it means general."

"Like the commander."

Joey nodded. "It's the only piece that can jump other pieces to escape capture."

Ellen was impressed with how much Joey knew. Listening, she knew no one would question if his midnight friend was real.

Joey continued, "Shaz says it's a military strategy game. Roman soldiers used to play it at night around the campfire."

"Fascinating," said Ellen.

Joey picked up two stones. "We start by adding two pieces to the board—wherever you want to place them. You do that until all the pieces are played. I'll move first to show you how."

He placed two stones side by side to protect each other's flank.

Ellen smiled watching how much Joey was enjoying his game. She followed him, placing two of her own pieces.

With all the pieces placed, Joey explained, "Now we can start. You want to surround each dog so either I can't move, or you kill the dog. Whoever kills all their opponent's pieces first wins."

Joey offered Ellen a proud look. "Shaz says I would make a great general."

Ellen smiled. She was enjoying watching Joey have fun.

"I almost forgot. One last rule . . . You can only move pieces up and back or sideways, but not diagonal."

Now he looked serious. "Ready to start?"

Ellen grinned. "I am, and may the best dux general win!"

Joey clapped. "Yes!"

Back at Church

Al pulled into the church parking lot. It was already filling up with people coming for tonight's performance.

Karen noted all the cars. "Wow, the play must really be popular. It's still an hour before it starts and people are getting here."

Al nodded. "Hunter and Denèe have been saying how popular it is. How people come from all over Richmond for the church's Christmas production."

"It's a big church," Karen noted, surveying the multiple buildings.

"Wait until you see the inside decorated for Christmas. The kids are gonna love it."

Karen turned to Ray and Stephanie sitting in the backseat. "Kids, are you excited?" She grinned big.

"Yeah!" they answered in unison.

"Is a real camel going to be inside the church?" six-year-old Ray asked.

Karen gave an enthusiastic nod. "That's what I hear."

"Let's hurry in," said Al, parking. "Kids, bundle up, it's still freezing outside."

They hurried across the lot and entered the vestibule area. The first thing they saw as they entered the atrium-like foyer were the two giant twenty-foot-tall Christmas trees.

"Oh, my," said Karen. "Al, it really is beautifully decorated."

Max, who was waiting in the atrium, saw them and waved as he hurried over to meet them.

"Welcome." He spoke to the children, "Ready to watch a Christmas play with a real camel?"

Alex's and Maggie's eyes lit up. "Really?" asked Maggie.

"Our camel's name is Penelope, and she's been in our church Christmas plays for a long time."

"So, who's hungry? There's pizza being served in the fellowship hall. It's for the cast members, but we are welcome."

Karen looked at her children, who were nodding." We grabbed some fast-food on the way. Kids, are you still hungry?"

"Yay!" they answered.

Al spoke, "Karen, you and the kids go have fun. I've got to meet Wayne up at the sound booth. I'll see everybody later."

Al left. Max said to Karen, "Come on, I'll show you around. Then we'll head back to the fellowship hall for pizza."

Max led them through a hallway that led back to the fellowship hall.

Following Max, Karen said, "I can't thank you and Ellen enough for helping make this a memorable Christmas for the children. Al and I weren't sure how we were going to manage Christmas with Joey back in the hospital."

"We're enjoying getting to know your family, Karen. Just like I bet Ellen and Joey are hitting it off."

Karen smiled. "They were doing great when I left. I feel so much better with her being there to read to Joey."

They entered the fellowship hall. Across one table were several boxes of pizza. "Help yourself, kids," said Max.

After feeding the children pizza, they returned to get their seats. At seven sharp, the lights in the sanctuary dimmed. It was the signal for everyone to take their seats. The play was about to begin.

Mr. Wilson walked out onstage to speak to the audience. He surveyed the auditorium filled to capacity and smiled.

"Welcome, everyone, to what may be the most fascinating portrayal of the Christmas story we all visit each year in the gospels. We here at Westend Community Church are thrilled you have come to see this year's Christmas production. Tonight, you will experience the Christmas story you all know, but in a new way. Fresh characters with drama the gospels only briefly talk about. You might call it the story behind the story. And while it's called a legend—because it's not official history—nevertheless, you may find yourselves believing this legend, as many of us already do.

"I want to give special recognition to one of our college student members. Hunter Reid, whose parents and grandparents have been members of Westend Community Church for as long as our church has put on these productions. Hunter is majoring in Special Arts at one of our local universities. Through the most unusual of events—a story to be told another time—Hunter came across an old, worn book and turned it into a play. That was last summer. Since then, he has given untold hours to this production. Again, thank you everyone for joining us tonight. Enjoy the adventurous story. I guarantee you will never think of the first Christmas the same ever again."

With that, the lights dimmed, and Mr. Wilson left the stage just as the curtains opened to reveal the first scene.

Children's Hospital

Ellen looked at her watch. It was after nine o'clock. The play was over, or close to it by now. She and Joey had played the ancient board game for an hour. Afterward, she had started reading *Legend of the Wooden Star*, which she had brought to read to Joey.

She had gotten to the part where Joseph, Mary, and baby Jesus had been discovered by one of Herod's soldiers while the family hid in an olive grove. That was when Joey had dozed off.

Ellen had then lowered his bed back to the horizontal position. He was not looking good. The last thing she wanted to do was wake him. He could finish hearing the story tomorrow—either from Karen or her, if she turned out to be watching her son. Watching Joey now, Ellen could see the boy had moved into the stage where his body would soon be losing its battle.

She looked past his bed to the star slowly twirling at the window. Whatever it meant—all the happenings around Joey's mysterious visitor—she could only hope that what he was telling Joey about searching for a miracle in the stars was real. However it might happen, she could see it needed to happen soon.

Before leaving, she laid a hand on Joey and said a prayer for his miracle. Then she gathered her things to leave. She left *Legend* on the tray table, where Karen would see it. She could hardly wait to meet Max at home to hear how opening night went.

Midnight

Shaz reached Joey's room. Looking up and down the quiet hall, he slipped inside. Walking over to the bed, he gazed down at Joey, who was asleep. No doubt, the effect of the painkiller. The medical monitors attached to the boy left no doubt of his crisis. That and Joey's ashen face showed a boy valiantly fighting for his life.

For a moment, Shaz pondered waking him. Then he decided against it. What was needed was a plan. Pondering what to do, his eye caught sight of the book lying next to the ancient board game. He reached down and picked it up. It had been a long time since he had seen a copy. It brought back memories.

Studying the leather-bound book, he had an idea. He pondered a moment, then with a nod, slipped the book into his satchel. Then he placed a hand on Joey and looked heavenward to say a prayer that there was still time enough to carry out what he was thinking.

Chapter 14

Saturday, midmorning
Children's Hospital

It was midmorning when Hunter and Denèe arrived at the Children's Hospital. Hurrying across the parking lot, they entered the hospital lobby. Security had tightened since the brouhaha started over Joey's midnight guest. Now hospital security was scrutinizing everyone, requiring they sign in and show ID.

Reaching the cancer ward floor, they approached the nurse's station. By now, the nursing staff all knew them.

"How's Joey?" they asked, anxiously walking up to the station.

It was Nurse Shelley. "He's taken a turn." Her eyes said it all.

"Can we go in?" they asked.

She nodded. "He'll be glad to see you."

Denèe took Hunter's hand as they walked down the hall. Reaching Joey's room, they lightly knocked before cracking the door open. Karen was already there. She waved them to come in.

"Joey, guess who's here to see you?" Karen said, offering him a big smile.

Hunter and Denèe came over to Joey's bedside. They looked at Joey, then at each other. They didn't have to speak to convey the same thought. Joey was not looking good.

Denèe spoke, "How is our stargazer doing?"

He offered Denèe a weak smile.

Hunter added, "How's it going, champ?"

Joey looked in the direction of the gold foil star still hanging in the window. "I better find my miracle star soon." He offered a sad look. "Shaz didn't come to see me last night either."

Denèe frowned. "Maybe something came up?"

He shrugged and gave Denèe a look that said he was hurt. "I need him to help me."

"I'm sure he'll be back," Denèe offered encouragingly. Changing the subject, she asked, "Did you have fun last night with Hunter's grandmother?"

Joey brightened at that. "Oma's fun. After playing my game, we started reading the story."

Hunter scanned the room, wondering whether Oma left the book or took it with her. She took it. "Did Oma say if she's coming back tonight to read to you?"

Karen answered, "I'm staying with Joey tonight. We're hoping to get the okay to go up to the rooftop."

Hunter and Denèe both offered a big smile upon hearing that.

"There you go, champ," Hunter said.

"We don't know yet for sure," Karen cautioned.

Wanting to keep the conversation positive, Denèe asked, "What do you think of the story so far?"

"I like the shepherd boy Micah. I think I would have done that."

"Done what?" Denèe asked.

"Carved that star."

Joey was thoughtful. "At least he was outside, where he could see the star." He pointed at the window. "I can't see anything from in here. I hope Dr. Ellie gets permission to take me up to the rooftop. There's a playground that's out in the open."

"That sounds exciting, Joey." Denèe looked at Karen for confirmation.

"That's what we're hoping too," Karen answered.

Just then, there was a brief knock at the door. Denèe and Hunter turned to see who it was. A female doctor walked in. She looked young, in her mid-twenties.

"I'm Elizabeth Stern, Joey's resident doctor." She walked over to them. "My kids here call me Dr. Ellie."

Denèe offered a handshake. "I'm Denèe, and this is my boyfriend, Hunter."

"He's been telling me all about you and your play."

She turned to Joey. "And this young fella here is my hero. Joey's the bravest kid I've seen in a long time."

Denèe shot Joey a big smile. "Hunter and I are his biggest fans too."

Dr. Ellie looked at the tray table where Game of Mercenaries was set up, ready to play. "This game, it's the same game as in your play, I hear?"

They nodded.

"Incredible. I'm from Israel. I recall hearing the name while visiting a museum in Jerusalem. It's so mysterious how it got here."

"We feel the same," Denèe said, looking at Hunter.

Hunter nodded. "We're certain there's a connection with all this. We just haven't figured out yet what that is."

Dr. Ellie turned to Joey and changed the subject. "I have exciting news!"

Joey's eyes grew big. "They said yes?"

Dr. Ellie offered a high-five. "Yep. Head doctor said okay."

Joey suddenly came to life. "Did you hear that, Mom? I can finally find my Miracle Star!"

Legend of the Wooden Star

Joey looked happier than Denèe and Hunter had seen him look since they met.

Denèe clasped her hands, excited. "That's wonderful, Joey!"

"Who of the staff will go with him?" Karen asked.

"I plan to go," Dr. Ellie answered. "Nurse Shelley wants to go. Plus, one of the aides will help wheel him up there."

She turned to Denèe and Hunter. "Wish you could go, but you have your play tonight, right?"

Hunter answered, "Wish we could too. Tonight is the second performance."

Dr. Ellie nodded that she understood. "I know Joey will want to tell you all about it." She turned to her young patient, giving him an affirming pat. "I'm excited that you can finally search for that special star!"

The excitement on Joey's face said it all.

Joey turned and gazed out the window at the overcast sky. "I hope the stars are shining tonight." He looked back at them. "It's my only chance to discover my miracle star."

No one said anything. They knew Joey was right.

Chapter 15

Saturday, early evening
Hospital rooftop

Karen had stayed with Joey throughout the afternoon. Now, picking up her cell phone, she checked the time. Six o'clock. Dr. Ellie had said that sometime after six, they would go up to the rooftop.

Looking out the window, Karen could see that the streetlights were on. Snow bounced off car headlights. Snow falling. That meant an overcast sky. She cringed. It was the last thing her son needed right now.

She looked back at Joey. He was asleep. Out of it, was more like it. His breathing labored. Clearly, his body was struggling to function. Just the sight of her boy in that state stabbed Karen's heart like cold steel.

Just then, Dr. Ellie cracked the door and peeked inside. "Are we ready?" she asked.

Karen nodded. "I think so. He's out of it, though."

Dr. Ellie acknowledged with a nod. "I'm not surprised. By the way, I went up to the rooftop a short while ago. The cloud cover is starting to break up." Clearly, Dr. Ellie was trying to sound hopeful.

Karen forced herself to be positive. "I hope so."

"Nurse Shelley will come along. She insisted on not missing tonight. She changed her shift to be with Joey."

Karen smiled. "I'm happy to hear that. Joey is quite attached to her."

"Joey is special to all the staff." Dr. Ellie added, "Also, Sol, one of our aides, will move Joey onto a gurney to carry him to the roof."

"You still planning to join us?" Karen asked.

"I wouldn't dare miss it. I'm honestly curious about this special star. Especially with all the news about a rare astronomical event that they are calling the Bethlehem Star."

"That's what we're hearing too. It all feels so mysterious. I attended the opening performance last night with my younger children. You maybe heard, the *Legend* story the play is based on revolves around the Bethlehem Star."

"I've only heard bits and pieces. You know, I grew up in Jerusalem, which is only ten kilometers from there."

Karen shook her head. "I didn't know that."

Dr. Ellie nodded. "The story in your gospels about Jesus's birth, while I'm Jewish, is so tied to my ancestry that I find this all quite interesting. Especially this mysterious visitor friend of Joey's. What do you make of that?"

Karen looked at the game resting on the tray table. "Clearly, there's a connection to all this. Al and I can't figure what that is. Even Denèe and Hunter are trying to solve it."

Dr. Ellie nodded. "I enjoyed chatting with them this morning. They make a nice couple. Joey sure seems attached."

Karen nodded.

"Speaking of Joey's midnight friend, wouldn't it be great if he showed up to join us?"

Karen agreed. "I was thinking the same. Especially after two nights ago when Shaz—what Joey calls him—brought charts that Joey says shows where to look in the sky."

Dr. Ellie's eyes grew wide. "So, he visited again? I hadn't heard. And still no reports from security. Not from the guard they have posted, or the cameras in the halls." Dr. Ellie made a face. "I have to tell you, this whole stranger visiting your son after hours has the hospital corporate all in a tizzy."

"It's had Al and me feeling the same. Not so much Joey's safety, as the stranger means Joey well, but just the idea it could happen and security none the wiser."

"Exactly." Dr. Ellie nodded.

There was another knock at the door. This time, an elderly Filipino man came in wheeling a gurney.

"Come in, Sol." Dr. Ellie waved. "Meet Karen Haskins, Joey's mom."

They greeted each other, then Sol asked, "Are you ready for me to move him onto the gurney?"

"It will wake him," Karen said. "But, believe me, he wouldn't miss this for anything."

A few minutes later, Nurse Shelley had joined them and helped roll Joey onto the elevator. By now, he was awake, his face filled with anticipation.

Riding up the elevator, he asked, "Will we see the stars?"

"That's what we're hoping," Nurse Shelley answered.

Joey frowned. "Dr. Ellie said she was coming too."

Nurse Shelley explained, "She is, said she'd be right up. Another child down from your room needed her." She added, "Dr. Ellie wants to be there when you spy your miracle star!"

Reaching the top floor, the elevator doors opened. While Karen and Nurse Shelley followed, the aide rolled Joey through double glass doors that opened onto the outdoor park.

Karen's eyes swept the area. There was a set of swings, a slide, a small merry-go-round, and other outdoor mechanical rides. A Japanese garden greeted them as they entered the park. Large urns filled with greenery were positioned along the entrance. Nothing was blooming this time of year. Overhead, a roof covered the entrance area. Beyond that, the park opened to the sky.

Karen was impressed. "This really is charming. Do the children use it a lot?"

Nurse Shelley nodded. "Especially so in warm weather. The kids and their parents love coming up here."

The double doors opened behind them. It was Dr. Ellie. "Hey, everybody, what do you think?"

"Charming," said Karen.

"And cold," Nurse Shelley added. "We need to make this happen quickly." She nodded at Joey, who already was shivering.

While Karen and the nurse had bundled Joey up as much as they could, it did not change how vulnerable he was to the elements, and it was freezing cold tonight.

"I'm okay," Joey answered bravely. "Take me out from under the roof so I can see the sky."

Sol guided the gurney into the open park area.

Joey's expression quickly went from anticipation to disappointment. A grey overcast sky blocked out the stars, except for a few small openings. Not enough to see the stars they knew, above the clouds, filled the night sky.

"I can't see much."

Karen asked, trying to be helpful, "Where did your friend Shaz say to look?"

"Shaz said to look in the direction the sun sets. He said it would appear low in the sky at first, then move up higher in the sky."

"The sun sets in this direction," Nurse Shelley said, rotating the front of the gurney so it pointed due west.

While the hospital was higher than the surrounding downtown buildings, the other buildings now blocked seeing anything on the horizon.

"Why did it have to snow?" Joey muttered to himself. He searched a full 180 degrees to the left and right of due west.

While Joey strained to see any sign of stars, Karen looked at Dr. Ellie and Nurse Shelley. Both showed looks of disappointment, like herself. She could feel her son's disappointment quickly building too.

Finally, he shook his head, his lips quivering. Karen wasn't sure whether from emotion or the cold.

"Maybe tomorrow night will be better?" He looked at Dr. Ellie. "Can we try to do this again? Tomorrow night is Christmas Eve. That's when Shaz says the miracle star will be brightest." His voice was hopeful.

Dr. Ellie's voice was understanding. "I'll find out. I know this is important."

Nurse Shelley motioned for Sol to turn the gurney back in the direction of the entrance. "Let's get Joey out of this cold!"

The aide quickly guided the gurney through the double doors and back into the hospital where it was warm.

Joey now surprised them with his next question. "Dr. Ellie, can you please let me go see the play tomorrow night? I'd rather do that than come up here again."

Karen cringed. She feared her son was giving up on finding his miracle star.

Dr. Ellie nodded. "If that's what you want, I'll find out."

He smiled, then closed his eyes. The exertion of coming up to the park had exhausted him.

Chapter 15

Westend Church
Following the night's performance

While the auditorium emptied as people headed home, Hunter and Denèe were in the back where the cast was changing back into their street clothes. At the same time, Miss Cho and her girls were organizing everything for tomorrow night.

Josh saw them and came over. "How do you think it went?" he asked.

Denèe answered, "Judging by the applause, the audience loved it."

Hunter added, "Fortunately, there was no last-minute crisis tonight, like last night."

Denèe explained, "Josh, you heard about the flat tire that almost kept Penelope from making the show?"

Josh nodded. "Yeah, I heard about that."

Hunter gave his friend a friendly pat on the arm. "You're doing a great job. Only one to go. Keep it up."

Denèe added, "Coming from Hunter, that means a five-star rating."

Josh grinned. "Tell me about it."

Hunter scanned the room. "Any chance you've seen Caelum?"

"Not since the play ended. Why?"

"We want him to visit Joey, who we've been telling you about. He's not doing well."

Josh made a face. "Sorry to hear that. If I see Caelum, I'll tell him you're looking for him."

Watching Josh walk off, Denise said, "I wonder if Joey got up to the hospital rooftop tonight? If he did, did he see his miracle star?"

Hunter nodded. "I was thinking that too. Maybe shoot Karen a text to find out?"

"Good idea." Denise pulled out her cell phone and instantly sent a text.

"While you check with her, I'm going to try to find Caelum. I really want him to visit Joey."

"Tonight?" Denèe asked.

"Yes, if we can. I keep feeling that Caelum can help Joey discover his star."

"By star, you mean the Great Conjunction event happening?" Denèe corrected.

"Yes. And there's only tonight and tomorrow night left."

Without saying so, they both knew that however Joey's star search turned out, he was quickly needing a miracle.

Story transitions to Amsterdam, Holland

Chapter 17

Amsterdam, Holland
Middle of the night before Christmas Eve day

The rector sat in his reading chair, where he had not moved for the past three hours, unable to put down what he was reading. He stayed entranced by the story. Truly, a remarkable story of what might have happened behind the scenes of the well-known events surrounding Jesus's birth.

While the story was true to the account, as told in the gospels, it introduced characters otherwise lost to history. Or never were, if the story was indeed fiction. Never mind, it was a fascinating account of the Biblical events, told through the eyes of a most unexpected character. A teenage shepherd boy was present that first Christmas night, attending the nativity with his shepherd family. A character who played a pivotal role in life of Jesus, even to the end of his ministry.

How the rector had come by the book he was reading was its own mystery. It had been three in the morning when he was in his study, preparing his message for tonight's Christmas Eve service. A message he had struggled with for inspiration.

Then had come a knock at the outside door. When he went to see who could be disturbing him at that hour, he had opened the door to find no one there. Only a still night, muffled by falling snow, and the wind sweeping the snow across the walkway leading down to the street.

He had looked up and down the street, only to find not a soul in sight. He had scanned the yard again just to be sure. There was definitely no one there. Neither were there any tracks in the snow showing that someone had been there. It gave him the strangest feeling.

Now, left to assume it was only the wind he had heard, he was about to close the door and return to his study. That was when he noticed the package on the stoop. So, someone had in fact knocked. Again, giving a quick scan down to the street, he had picked up the package and carried it back to his study.

Curious, of course, he had unwrapped the plain brown paper. Inside was a book. Leather bound. Clearly old from its condition. The book's title, in faded letters, read *Legend of the Wooden Star*.

At the same time, no mention of an author. So, penned anonymously. Even more curious, who could have left the book at his doorstep in the middle of the

Legend of the Wooden Star

night? His curiosity aroused by then, he had taken the book over to his reading chair, settled in, and began. Soon, he was captivated by the story.

In fact, he was so entranced that he had sat for three hours not moving, until he had read the entire story. Now it was six o'clock in the morning. The city was still not awake. What an extraordinary account, he sat there thinking. If true, it brought to life the scenes as told in the gospels. It gave behind-the-scenes details of what happened that night when King Herod's soldiers descended on Bethlehem. Slaughtering—according to historians—as many as twenty boy toddlers under the age of two. An incident so briefly told as to easily move on to the next scene in the Gospel account—that being the Christ child's family's escaping to Egypt.

But how had that happened, practically speaking? The *Legend* told in detail how it happened. And who was involved. It was told with such vivid detail that the rector knew he would never again read the Gospel account the same way. All as seen in the first person by a twelve-year-old shepherd boy who, along with his shepherd family, had visited the nativity. It was just how the Gospels described it happening.

But what the Gospels didn't tell was the harrowing escape by the family, aided by the shepherd boy introduced at the beginning, with the help of the Magi's mysterious servant. From that fateful night, fast-forward thirty-three years later to the end of Jesus's ministry, when that same shepherd boy reemerged. This time, with the most shocking identity the rector could ever have imagined.

Was it possible the story was true? He couldn't be sure, because there was no historical account to back it up. It was why the book's title called it a "legend." Still, the characters felt so real. He could easily believe the events happened that way. But it was the ending that most touched him—what the Bethlehem Star's secret message was.

Satisfied that he had the perfect message for tonight, he lifted out of his reading chair and carried the book over to his desk. Now, with nothing blocking his inspiration, he began to write.

Transition back to Richmond

Chapter 18

Children's Hospital
Leading up to the final performance

It was five o'clock. Earlier that afternoon, Dr. Ellie had come into Joey's room with the news that the department heads had decided to grant Joey's wish. Dr. Ellie had gone to bat for him after the disappointment of last evening on the rooftop park.

Arrangements were made for an ambulance to transport Joey to Westend Community Church for the final performance. After the disappointment of not seeing the miracle star, his mood was again exuberant. Finally, he was attending Hunter and Denèe's church play.

The change of mood had relieved both Karen and Al. They knew deep down, in unspoken words, that it was the hospital giving their son his last wish. Karen had stayed with Joey to ride in the ambulance, while Al brought Stephanie and Ray with him to the church. Ellen, always helpful, had volunteered to help with the children while Al focused on sound booth duties.

To get Joey ready for the special night, Karen had dressed him in his Sunday best. Just now, she had finished fitting him out in a red Christmas sweater and dress slacks. She stood back, admiring.

"Don't you look snazzy."

"Oh, Mom." He gave the typical boy's reaction to a compliment about how he looked.

She glanced at her phone. "Your ride should be here any minute."

Too weak to ride in a wheelchair, he was transported by gurney, both to the ambulance, then into the church, where he would remain during the play.

"Are you excited?" She already knew the answer.

Talking tired him. Still, he mustered up the effort. "I can't wait, Mom."

Just then, a knock at the door. It was the aide, Sol, who had arrived with the gurney.

Karen offered Sol a smile. "We're ready."

An hour later, the ambulance pulled into the church parking lot, then under the portico used for unloading passengers. With the help of ushers already expecting Joey's arrival, they helped wheel him into the church atrium.

Karen had the ushers pause so Joey could view the two twenty-foot-tall live Christmas trees standing on either side of the entrance doors leading into the sanctuary. They looked magnificent reaching to the high ceiling. Karen's heart danced as she watched her son's eyes grow round with wonder as he gazed at the trees.

"What are those cards hanging on the branches?" he asked.

Karen answered, "Those are the names of children who have a parent in prison. The church has committed to bringing each of the children a special Christmas."

She turned to the two ushers standing by. "Can you show us where you want Joey to be positioned?"

"Yes, ma'am," the high-school-age ushers said. Opening the wide doors leading into the sanctuary, they wheeled Joey behind the pews set up for wheelchairs.

Already there in the auditorium, Ellen and Max saw Karen and Joey come in. They waved and hurried over.

"Hello, Joey." Ellen offered him a big smile. "We were so excited to hear you were coming tonight!" She turned to Max. "Joey, this is Hunter's grandfather. You can call him Opa, like Hunter does. And me, of course, Oma."

"It's a pleasure to finally meet you, Joey," Max said, gently shaking Joey's limp hand.

Ellen turned to the young ushers standing by to help. "Will you please let Hunter know that Joey has arrived?"

They nodded and headed toward backstage.

Ellen turned to Karen. "While we wait for Hunter and Denèe to come say hi, I want you to meet Hunter's folks. She pointed to the couple nearby chatting with another couple.

"I'll bring them over," Max volunteered.

Introductions made, Scott Reid, Hunter's dad, said, "We've been hearing about some rather mysterious happenings going on at the hospital. Is it true you have a midnight visitor who nobody but you sees?"

Joey nodded yes.

Ashley chuckled. "Hunter's been giving us brief details. That is, when he slows down long enough to share."

"We hear that," Max seconded.

Karen spoke, "Your son and his girlfriend have been so wonderful visiting Joey. Haven't they, Joey?"

Joey nodded. "Even playing my new game with me."

"Game of Mercenaries..." Scott pondered aloud. "That brings back memories of reading the *Legend* book."

Legend of the Wooden Star

Joey added, "Oma and I got to the part where the game was used to bribe Herod's soldier. It's really cool that my game is in the story."

Ellen gave a nod. "Did you get a chance yet to read any more of the story? I left the book on the tray table."

Karen looked surprised to hear that. "No one has seen it since you were there Friday night."

Ellen looked surprised. "I left it in plain sight on the tray table next to the game." She added, "I hope nothing has happened to it. It's a family keepsake."

Karen looked as perplexed as Ellen. "This is so strange." She turned to Joey. "Could your friend have borrowed it?"

Joey shook his head no. "Mom, Shaz hasn't visited me for two nights now."

Ellen looked disappointed. "Do you think one of the nurses might have borrowed it? They must be curious with everything being talked about."

"I will ask when we get back," Karen promised.

Scott added a positive note. "In the meantime, Hunter has turned the book into a play. From what I hear, it sounds to be more exciting than the book."

Ashley nodded proudly. "We heard that Mr. Wilson wants to send the script to some agents he knows up in New York for, perhaps, a Broadway production."

"That is exciting," said Karen.

Just then, Hunter and Denèe entered the auditorium. Seeing everyone, they hurried up the aisle.

Denèe gave Joey a hug. "You made it. I'm so happy!"

"Glad you could come, champ," Hunter added, offering a fist bump.

Joey grinned big. Everyone could see how attached he was to the couple.

Hunter looked at his folks. "Mom, Dad, you've obviously met Joey. Right now, we can't stay to visit, but you all enjoy talking." Hunter was about to leave, then stopped to turn back. "Where are Jenny and her girls?"

Ellen answered, "They're running late. We're saving them seats on our pew. You can see them after the play."

With that, Hunter headed at a double pace to wherever he was going. Denèe stayed back and called to Hunter, "I'll be there in a minute."

She frowned now, explaining, "We have a *huge* crisis on our hands. Caelum, who plays the Magi's servant Belteshazzar, hasn't showed up yet. And he's not answering his cell phone, either."

"Oh my," Ellen gasped. "What are you going to do?"

Denèe grimaced. "Hunter's going to get dressed for the part. No one else knows the lines like him."

"Wow!" Scott whistled. "That is a genuine crisis."

Denèe gently stroked Joey's arm. "We'll see you after the show." She paused and added, "Tell Hunter's folks about your midnight friend."

"Okay," said Joey, watching her leave.

"Enjoy the performance," she called back as she hurried off.

Max looked at his watch. "We have about twenty minutes before curtain time. For Hunter's sake, I sure hope this Caelum character shows up."

Everyone agreed.

Ellen changed the subject. "I'm going to get Ray and Stephanie."

She had left them to enjoy refreshments in the fellowship hall, goodies the kitchen had prepared for the cast and crew. One of the ladies working kitchen duty had volunteered to keep an eye on the children. Ellen thought that far better than them having nothing to do while the adults visited.

"I'll go with you," Karen offered.

Ellen turned to Scott and Ashley. "Wait till you hear about Joey's midnight friend. Scott, it will make you think of Zachery."

Back in Amsterdam . . .

Chapter 19

Christmas Eve service

Christmas Eve was promising a white Christmas. Snow had begun falling earlier that evening. While a snowfall was not unusual for a Holland winter, it happened infrequently enough to be special. For Rudi Hogenboom, any snowy evening was an enjoyable time to stroll the streets. The city was quieter, with falling snow muting the usual noises. It allowed him to think without distractions. Also, there was something about snow falling at night, floating past the streetlights and lit houses, that created a surreal feeling Rudi found comforting. Impressionistic, like a Monet painting. Tonight, hoping the snowfall would lift his spirits, he had ventured out for a walk along the streets.

Rudi had left his apartment a half-hour earlier, when the snowfall began. Already, Prinsengracht Street, where he was strolling along the Canal District, was covered with new snow. Even the canal he now walked along had frozen over from the cold snap. Boats now set motionless, moored along the edges of the canal.

In fact, all the city canals had frozen over. An unusual occurrence, which in turn had drawn out the children with their skates. All afternoon he had watched them from his apartment window, playing games or racing up and down the canal. He had hoped their gaiety would help his despondency. It hadn't. Not today on the first anniversary of his loss. Even the solitude of tonight's walk only heightened his feelings of depression

A year ago, Rudi had lost his grandson Hans to leukemia. They had said goodbye on Christmas Eve. The young boy had waged a valiant fight. This form of cancer was aggressive, requiring his last remaining hope—a modern-day medical miracle—called a bone marrow transplant.

Neither Rudi nor any of the other family members, as tests turned out, were an acceptable match for Hans. Nor had the International Donor Bank produced a donor. At least one who was willing to follow through with the transplant procedure. Rudi grimaced. That was the hardest part to accept. The donor bank had found a match, only to learn the potential donor had decided not to donate. It was Hans's last hope.

As he passed row houses and shops that lined both sides of the canal, Rudi weaved his way through throngs of parked bicycles, useless in snow. He recalled back to Hans's last Christmas. Back to December fifth, the

St. Nicholas celebration. As was the custom for Dutch children, Hans had set a wooden shoe outside the front door. It was a signal for Sinterklaas to stop and leave a special treat. The same scene was multiplied across the city with households who had children.

The next morning had brought Hans not just the usual treats, but a mysterious gift. A hand-carved wooden star the size of an open palm. While the craftsmanship was amateurish, still it was easily recognizable as a star. It looked old; the grain was worn smooth from years of handling. Stranger still, on the backside of the star, along the long tail, were letters carved into the wood. The symbols were from an alphabet neither Rudi nor the rest of the family recognized.

Baffled, no one in the family claimed to leave it. Neither did the neighbors, who Rudi asked. But Rudi's eleven-year-old grandson Hans knew. It was from Sinterklaas. St. Nicholas had brought him his very own Christmas Star!

That night, his grandson had asked Rudi to read the Christmas story again. He especially wanted to hear the part about the Magi being led by the special star to Bethlehem. And the shepherds who were visited by an angel and Heavenly Host and then had visited baby Jesus in the manger.

The memory of that final night with Hans caused Rudi to tear up. Afterward, Hans had asked Rudi questions about Heaven. Where was Heaven exactly? What was it like? When he died, would the angels come to get him to take him there? Honest forthright questions only a child would ask.

He tried to answer Hans's questions as best he could. All the while, struggling with his own questions. Mostly, why God would take Hans's last hope to survive his leukemia. Try as he may, Rudi could not reconcile this failure on God's part. That is, if there was a God up there who really cared. Which is what Rudi now questioned.

That next week, Hans was admitted to the hospital. Finally, his last night had come. During their chat, Hans's voice was so weak that Rudi had to draw close to hear him speak. Then Hans had closed his eyes and gone to sleep. All the while, peacefully clutching his little wooden star, the same way he did every night. The next morning, Hans was gone.

Recalling that final night, Rudi stopped to gaze up at the night sky. Snowflakes landed on his face and in his eyes. Whether it was from tears or the snow, he wiped them away. The overcast sky and falling snow blocked out the stars that ordinarily would be shining. He thought about the special star he had read about from the Bible to his grandson. A star that had announced hope and peace and goodwill to mankind. None of which he felt. Nor had he felt it over the past year. Even if the stars had been shining tonight, he knew there would be no special star up there shining down hope. In fact, Rudi no longer believed in that special star. It was a nice story. That was all.

He turned his eyes from the sky to the street as he walked on. There was something else he was struggling with. After being tested as a match for his grandson, the results had gone into the International Donor Bank. A week ago, he had learned he was a match for someone in the United States. Was Rudi willing to go through with the procedure? the agency had asked. Rudi had declined. Why should he? The system had let down his grandson. Still, the decision not to offer life to someone was weighing heavily on Rudi now. He couldn't shake the feeling of guilt. Especially the thought that it could be a young child Hans's age.

Up ahead, he spied the famous Westerkerk Church. As he neared, he could see through the windows. The inside was lit up. The traditional Christmas Eve service was taking place inside. Reaching the Kerk, he paused. He gazed up at the 300-foot spire reaching far into the sky. A landmark in the city.

What was it? He could feel a tugging inside to go in. There was nothing happening that he wanted to see or hear inside, he told himself. He was over those feelings. Trying to walk on, he stopped, turned, and gazed back at the church. Before all this had happened with Hans, one of Rudi's most cherished memories was Christmas Eve services. That now felt like another lifetime.

He stood, unable to move, his legs feeling frozen. He felt himself fighting conflicting emotions. What was it? As if on autopilot, he started moving toward the church, then began climbing the steps to the large front doors. Pulling one open, as if somehow in a dream, he entered the grand church anterior. Sure enough, a candlelight service was in progress. Quietly, he slipped through another set of doors into the sanctuary and found a seat in the back, where he started to listen.

The minister standing in the traditional raised pulpit was telling the congregation about a most unusual experience he had the night before. While preparing for his message, there had come a knock at his office door. When he went to see, there was only wind and swirling snow. That was when he noticed a small package on the stoop. Curious, he had brought it inside. The package was wrapped in plain brown paper, with no name addressed on the outside or postage showing that it was delivered by the mail carrier.

When the rector had unwrapped the package, inside he found a worn leather-bound book titled *Legend of the Wooden Star*. Its author was anonymous. He had begun reading and soon found himself caught up in the suspenseful account surrounding the first Christmas. But it was the story's ending that most

Legend of the Wooden Star

touched the rector. How that final day when the shepherd boy Micah, now a grown man, would once again see Jesus thirty-three years later.

When Mary had returned the little wooden star to Micah, while standing near the cross where Jesus hung, the little wooden star took on a new meaning. The star he had carved resembled not just a special star, but the Cross.

Rudi knew the message tonight was for him. Somewhere during the telling, he had taken Hans's little wooden star from his coat jacket. Studying it as he listened to the rector, Rudi wondered, *Was what he was thinking possible?*

Thinking how Hans's wooden star mysteriously showed up on the doorstep, Rudi thought he understood. The star was a gift for Hans. Who delivered it, Rudi would never know. But for Hans, it was a message that Heaven was waiting for him. That soon, little Hans would be going up to the stars. It was not a sad picture, but a hopeful one. Hans had made the transition. Rudi, left behind, had not. Hans's last words were for his grandfather to give the little wooden star to the next boy or girl who needed that same hope.

Following the service and the singing of "Silent Night," Rudi made his way down to the front, to where there was a life-size creche with shepherds and Wise Men kneeling beside the manger. Overhead was the Christmas star with its long tail pointed down to the famous scene. Taking Hans's wooden star that he was holding, Rudi laid it in the manger next to the baby Jesus figure. Then he looked upward, where he could imagine Hans now was looking down, pleased with what his grandfather was doing.

Rudi was gifting the hand-carved star to the Christ child. Just as the shepherd boy had done that first Christmas night. He knew it was what Hans would do if he were there. As to his lingering question *why*, Rudi now realized faith was the bridge from life on earth to eternity. Finally, he could celebrate that his Hans was with the angels in Heaven.

While he couldn't change what happened to Hans with his donor, Rudi knew he didn't want the same on his conscience. With resolve, knowing what he must do, he headed for the exit. Somewhere, a life hung in the balance that he could save. Perhaps a child Hans's age.

Meanwhile, standing quietly in the back, a tall Middle Eastern man watched. His eyes followed the Dutchman making his way up the aisle to the exit. As Rudi passed by, the tall stranger offered an approving nod. Now his gaze turned to the creche down front. There was a young boy who he knew was waiting for his miracle. A miracle that small wooden star could help make happen.

He allowed himself a satisfied smile. Where he had failed a year ago to bring a miracle, tonight would be different. Tonight, that boy, along with his parents, would celebrate a joyful Christmas Eve.

Back at Westend Community Church...

Hunter was in the dressing area with Mrs. Cho, who was frantically trying to put together what Hunter needed to wear to play Belteshazzar.

She held up the costume Caelum was meant to be wearing. "He's much taller than you. Miss Cho has to fix it quickly."

As she turned to head for her sewing table, Caelum dashed in. Seeing the situation, he said, "That won't be necessary. I'm here."

"Caelum, where have you been?" Hunter wasn't sure whether to be angry or thrilled.

"My apologies. My business waylaid me. But I'm here, and I do believe I have a bit of time to get ready before my entrance."

Hunter relaxed. "Okay, I'm glad you made it. I was in a bit of a tizzy."

Just then, Denèe walked in. "Caelum, thank goodness you made it!" She walked over and wrapped an arm around Hunter's waist. "You had our director in a tizzy."

"So I hear." Caelum smiled. "All good now. Let me get ready."

Miss Cho handed Caelum his outfit. "It's ready." Shaking her head, she headed to the next costume fitting.

Hunter looked at Denèe. "How are things backstage?"

"I just came from there. First scene is ready." She looked at her Apple watch. "Mr. Wilson should be coming on stage in seven minutes. Follow through with your plan tonight."

Denise meant how the previous two nights, Hunter had served as stage manager.

Hunter placed his hands on his hips, looking decisive. "Know what? Tonight, I think I will treat myself and go sit out in the audience and watch the show, like everybody else."

Denèe smiled. "I like that. Why don't you sit with your family? They have a full pew. If I can, I will join you. But before that happens, I want to get us through the first two to three scenes."

Hunter blew her a kiss. "Try to break a leg without me." He chuckled, heading to the sanctuary.

Legend of the Wooden Star

By the time Hunter reached the pew, the lights had already dimmed. He slid in next to his Oma.

She gave a surprised look. "I wasn't expecting your company."

He winked. "I'm treating myself, Oma."

Max leaned over and whispered, "So I take it Caelum made it?"

Hunter nodded. "Yes, barely."

"Well, enjoy," Ellen said. "You've worked hard to get to tonight."

Now Mr. Wilson walked onstage to speak to the audience, the same as he did on the previous nights. He repeated what he said before, except adding that tonight was extra special. It was Christmas Eve.

What Mr. Wilson said next, Hunter wasn't expecting.

"We have with us tonight a very special guest. He's just come from the Children's Hospital downtown. Over the past week, Joey Haskins and his family from South Hill, Virginia, have become part of our family." He spotted the gurney. "Joey, we all want to wish you an especially enjoyable time. Tonight's performance is about a miracle star. What I believe you've been searching for."

Seated in the back where no one could see his reaction, Joey's face lit up. He looked at his mom seated next to him. "He's talking about me."

Karen smiled and patted his arm. "Yes, he is."

"That was a nice gesture that Mr. Wilson just made," Ellen whispered.

Hunter nodded. "I didn't know he was going to do that."

Like with each prior performance, the curtains opened to reveal the first scene. Hidden behind the curtains on either side of the stage were two narrators, Sheila Mae and and Ross, another local drama teacher. The two provided both a female and male voice to simulate the narrative.

Shepherds sat around a campfire, the flames produced by an electric log fire prop. Above the stage, a large dark blue blanket with holes cut out allowed for small LED lights to peek through, resembling twinkling stars. One star, far larger than the others, hung suspended above the shepherds, bathing them with its light.

The shepherds were in a heated discussion about the Roman occupation of Palestine, which for the Jews was their sacred Promised Land. When would God send Israel a messiah to drive out the Romans? One shepherd's voice rose above the others.

Legend of the Wooden Star

While the older men argued how that might happen, a young shepherd boy whittled on a piece of wood. The boy was played by Hunter's schoolmate Josh. His eyes switched back and forth from the brilliant star and the piece of wood he was whittling to resemble it.

The play had begun.

Part II
The Play

Legend of the Wooden Star

The air was crisp that spring night. The sky was clear of clouds, revealing a kaleidoscope of stars that spread across the vast backdrop of space, twinkling with varying intensities, creating a shimmering spectacle that extended from horizon to horizon as far as the eye could see. Palestine's open and mostly barren landscape offered the perfect setting for stargazers.

For anyone who wished to study the endless display of moving bodies that created amazing geometric configurations for the imaginative who gazed long enough. The configurations even transforming into images of men and animals. It was only natural to surmise that these images were placed there as symbols to tell a story. To reveal a mystery. Placed there by the Grand Master of Creation for mortals on earth to search and wonder. For truth seekers who searched the Heavens for answers. To seek the Divine for messages hidden in these moving bodies above. Even foretelling what was yet to come . . .

Tonight, in one of the fields in the outlying hill country of Judea, outside the small historic village of Bethlehem, a group of shepherds sit around their campfire for light and warmth. It is that time of year when the sheep are let out into the fields to graze and birth their ewes. Tonight is a typical night, no different from any other night. The spring no different this year than the year before. No doubt, from the next year yet to come. Except tonight, something is about to happen that will change history.

In that setting, a shepherd boy sits around the campfire with his father, uncles, and grandfather. Presently, his attention is fixed on an unusually bright star that appeared some fortnights ago. The boy was quick to notice its first appearance, as he was in the habit of studying the heavenly bodies at night with nothing more to do while guarding the sheep. This star is not just brighter and larger than any surrounding stars, it looks so close it feels like he could strike it with a stone thrown from his slingshot.

Since it first appeared, he had watched the star move closer to their camp. Finally, tonight it shined directly overhead. There was something mystifying about the star, and he wondered if it could be a sign of something important to come. Captivated, he decided to carve the star. He found a thick olive branch under a nearby ancient grove of olive trees. With the perfect piece of wood, he begun the task of carving the star's likeness.

While the boy, whose name is Micah, whittles, the older shepherds pay no notice. They are focused on a game that pits two opponents, each man taking his turn to play the last winner. It is a game popular with Roman soldiers and traveling merchants. Micah's Uncle Reuben has boasted how he acquired the game, called Game of Mercenaries, when his band ambushed a small group of Roman soldiers passing through the hill country.

Micah knows that Uncle Reuben is no ordinary thief, but a member of a revolutionary group called Zealots, dedicated to liberating Palestine from vlle, pagan Roman occupation. To his fellow Jews, Uncle Reuben is a folk hero, revered for his dangerous exploits and how he shares the bounty from successful ambushes with fellow Jews in need.

Tonight, Uncle Reuben has showed up unexpectedly, as he often does under the cover of darkness. He is wanted by the local Roman occupiers, dead or alive. Thus, his appearing clandestinely and unannounced. Uncle Reuben's men are known to patrol the open countryside, starting south of Jerusalem and extending through the hill country, down to nearby Bethlehem and beyond, down to the major east-west and north-south trade routes that intersect at the city of Hebron. Now, while the men play the Game of Mercenaries, Uncle Reuben boasts about his band's most recent exploit.

"My brothers, you should have been there to see. There we were, positioned behind the rocks overhead, offering a perfect view of the trail below that narrows as it passes through the tall rocks on either side." He pointed in the direction of the hill country located beyond the nearby olive grove.

"We know the area well," another uncle said, "go on with your story, Reuben."

Uncle Reuben continued, "We had already spied the small group of soldiers approaching. About a dozen men with several village boys carrying their packs, like the Roman pigs are always doing."

Uncle Reuben was speaking of the practice by Roman soldiers of snatching young boys as they passed through villages, ordering the boys to carry their packs as far as the next village, where they would repeat the practice on a new set of victims.

"It was a small enough unit that we could ambush and overwhelm the swine soldiers," Uncle Reuben spit his words. "Especially with surprise on our side. And that's what we did. As always, we used their own weapons on them. Swords and spears we had seized from other raids. But it is our deadly aim with our slingshots they fear most."

Micah was listening intently now. Just as were the others. Uncle Reuben's story was getting good.

"As the soldiers came close, we each selected a target. They outnumbered us, but we had the advantage of the high ground and the element of surprise. As they passed through the narrow strait of rocks, we attacked, striking them with deadly aim, hitting them in the face, neck, and other parts of their body not protected by helmet and armor. Pelted from all sides from above, they quickly surrendered. This time, we hit the mother lode. The soldiers were transporting salt and silver to the post down at Hebron to be used to pay the soldiers there. We absconded with enough to last our band for weeks."

"What about the boys carrying their packs?" Micah's father asked.

"After stripping the soldiers of their weapons and sending them on their way, we shared some of the booty with the boys, then released them to go back to their local village."

Micah's grandfather Mordecai now spoke. "We will suffer from this attack, Reuben. Especially with your ambush so close to our settlement. Roman soldiers will surely visit us and demand to know what we know. What shall we tell them?"

"Lie to them, Father. Tell them you know nothing and have nothing to do with this marauding band of thieves. Remember, it is the Romans who steal from us with their heavy taxes. They take the sword to anyone who dares to even challenge their actions when they come into our villages. We must stand against this tyranny any way we can."

"Reuben is right, Father," Micah's father agreed. "Until the God of our fathers delivers us by raising up a king like our mighty King David of old, we must defend ourselves as best we can."

"You are wrong, son," said Mordecai, gazing into the campfire. "The God of our fathers promised to never forsake his people. The scriptures tell us to wait upon the Lord. He is the God of our salvation."

Reuben scoffed at the words. "Is that to mean we are to do nothing to defend ourselves, Father? I think not. I would rather die than submit to these heathen Romans and to that despot King Herod."

Again, Grandfather Mordecai spoke. "Reuben, you are young and full of zeal, but I tell you this. Jehovah has promised to send his Chosen People a King. A King amongst kings. A King who will defend his people and restore the land that is rightfully ours, the land Jehovah promised to our father Abraham. It will be done according to the word of the prophets."

As he spoke, suddenly the campfire's flames came to life, rising into the night air several feet above their heads, causing the shepherds to leap back in fear.

What happened next strained the imagination. Amid the fire, Micah could make out a figure who was alive. Yes, there was no doubt. He seemed to float in the middle of the flames. A man in raiment even brighter than the fire itself, standing head and shoulders above even the tallest man.

Micah wanted to run but he couldn't move. Neither his father or uncles or grandfather moved either. They stood frozen, transfixed, as the being now spoke.

"Shepherds, men of Israel, listen to what I have to say! For tonight, I bring you incredible news . . . This King you were just speaking of is born this night in the nearby village of Bethlehem. His arrival foretold by the prophets. You must go seek him and pay homage. Even now, the child is with his parents in a cave behind the ancestral home of King David. You are favored, brave men. Chosen by Heaven to hear this news so that you might be the first to go and worship Israel's promised king, the savior of your people."

Micah felt as though he was in a dream as he listened. This being, whoever or whatever he was, was untouched by the blazing fire. His voice no ordinary voice, but that like the sound of mighty rushing waters. His raiment glowing. His eyes piercing. Brighter than the fire itself. As the being finished speaking, the night sky suddenly opened above them.

As the men looked on, a host of radiant beings, like the figure in the campfire, began to fill the night sky. An untold number. Moving in harmony to a heavenly music playing somewhere. Everywhere. Their voices melodious as they sang praises to the highest God, who tonight had answered the cry of his people. They sang in a language Micah somehow understood. The voices and the music was like nothing ever heard by man on earth.

Micah and the others stood transfixed. So, this was what Heaven was like . . . the music, the pageantry of the figures swirling in perfect symmetry in the night sky. A euphoria now flooded Micah's being as he watched the display of heavenly hosts celebrate. His senses told him it was real. Still, it felt beyond imagination.

The heavenly display went on with no sense of time. Then finally, as if on cue, the beings began to ascend in a swirling configuration, pulling them higher, until they disappeared out of sight. Just as suddenly as they had appeared, they were gone, and the night sky became dark once again, except for the stars. The campfire had returned to subdued embers. Micah noticed how that brightest of stars he had followed for several nights on, now shone even more brightly. Somehow, that star that had appeared played into what he had just witnessed, of that he was certain.

For the longest moment, no one spoke. The men stood fixated around the fire. None had moved throughout the event. As if recovering from a paralysis, they now looked around their surroundings, uncertain. Their gazes locked on one another, eyes wide with wonderment. Finally, it was Grandfather Mordecai who spoke.

"My sons, this night we have been visited by Heaven's angels. You heard what these beings said. The Angel of God inside the fire. A Child King is born tonight. Our Messiah has come. Now, we must obey and go to see this child for ourselves."

"Do we know where to go, Grandfather?" asked Micah, tucking the wooden star he had finished carving into his belt.

"The angel mentioned King David's ancestral home," Micah's father answered. "Do we know which house that is?"

The men gazed in the direction of Bethlehem, the village now asleep in the distance, less than an hour's walk away.

"I am familiar with the ancestral home," Reuben answered. "It serves now as an inn for travelers. Follow me." He started off in the direction of the village.

"Who will watch the sheep?" Micah asked, looking out in the field where the family's sheep were huddled tightly together to stay warm.

Grandfather Mordecai answered, "None of us wants to be left behind. The sheep will be fine for a short while. Come, let us all go to see this child!"

An hour later, they entered the village, following a street to the end where King David's family home backed up to a hillside. Behind the house, Micah could see a light coming from a cave set into the hill. It served as a stable for animals.

The men exchanged an uncertain look, then without hesitating, headed to the lit cave.

As they neared, they could see the father standing watch over his young wife who lay on a makeshift bedding of straw, resting, the child in her arms. The first thing Micah thought was how the scene revealed nothing of the significance of what the angel being had announced. The parents and child were just ordinary people. But no one could deny what he and the others had just witnessed.

As they drew near, Reuben called out, "We have come to see your son after hearing the news!"

"What news is that?" the father replied, stepping warily outside the mouth of the cave.

"Israel's Messiah King."

"Let them come in, Joseph," the mother said to the father. "I want to hear what they have heard."

As the shepherds gathered inside the small cave, Micah listened while the men shared what they had just witnessed. They learned that the parent's names were Joseph and Mary, and the child they had named Yeshua. The parents were now asking the shepherds to share exactly what had transpired. When the men were finished, there was a long silence. Finally, Joseph spoke.

"Mary and I have had our own visitations from God, confirming what you just now shared. Yes, our son is the Messiah you speak of."

What the father said next surprised Micah.

"What is important now is that our son's identity does not get out to the public. These are dangerous times. Not just the Romans, but King Herod won't take kindly to any news that his rule over Judea could be in jeopardy. Can we ask that you keep what you have learned tonight a secret?"

Grandfather Mordecai answered for all of them. "You have our word. One of my sons, Reuben, is a Zealot. We are on the side of Israel, not our occupiers."

Joseph nodded. "That is good to hear."

The men wanted to know what they could do to help the family.

Joseph explained, "When my ancestor who manages the Inn hears what happened tonight, I believe he will invite us to move inside. You see," Joseph looked at Mary, "we have not yet been officially married, only betrothed."

The mother now spoke. "My child was not birthed the natural way of a man and woman. Joseph has never known me. I am still a virgin. How I came to bear Yeshua is a miracle itself."

Micah and the others listened in awe to the young mother.

"Then truly this child is of God," Grandfather Mordecai replied. He looked at his sons, then back at the parents. "I am afraid we brought nothing in the way of a gift to pay homage to Israel's king."

"Your sharing what you witnessed tonight is gift enough," said the father.

Micah reached for the wooden star in his belt. He held it up for all to see. "I carved this while gazing at the special star that appeared the past few nights," Micah explained as he handed the star to Joseph.

The other shepherds looked surprised. "So, that is what Micah was carving?"

Micah nodded.

Joseph accepted the wooden star and looked it over, then handed it to the mother.

She looked up at Micah and smiled. "It is a beautiful carving." She offered to give it back.

Micah shook his head. "No, I would like for you to have it. A gift from my family to the Messiah child."

"That is kind of you. What is your name?" the mother asked.

"Micah. I carved my name into the back of the star, thinking I would keep it."

"Micah, I will cherish this star as a reminder of this night. When little Yeshua is older, I will be sure to tell him of the events this night."

Micah beamed with pride.

Grandfather Mordecai gave a proud pat on his grandson's shoulder, then looked around at his sons. "Let us leave the parents now so they might get some rest." He spoke to the father, "We are in the fields, not far outside of town. Let us know if you need our help with anything."

The parents agreed, and the shepherds took their leave.

Walking back, Reuben was the first to speak, "Do you know what this means?"

Micah's father, Simeon, looked at his younger brother skeptically. "Tell us, Reuben."

"This means we will have to wait at least twenty years before this child is old enough to lead an army to defeat the Roman occupiers. I will be too old to fight by then. We all will except for Micah."

"Who said he came to fight?" Grandfather Mordecai asked, challenging his son.

"What else does a king do? A Messiah King."

The other brother Levi, who often didn't speak, nodded. "Reuben is right, Father. We will be many years under this tyranny, waiting for this child to become an adult."

Grandfather Mordecai, always the thoughtful one, answered, "You would challenge the wisdom of our God. After what you witnessed tonight! You all should be more careful. What we witnessed was sacred. And for some reason only our God knows, we were chosen to hear this news."

Micah watched as Rueben walked ahead. He could see his uncle was still not happy. Alas, that was the way of a revolutionary, Micah concluded.

Eight months later

The Roman pagan holiday Saturnalias, celebrated in December, has arrived.

Legend of the Wooden Star

That night, Micah is amazed when he looks up in the sky and sees the same bright star of that momentous night back in the spring. Once again, it appears to shine directly over Bethlehem. At once, he is elated and apprehensive. What could it mean? Something supernatural is about to happen again. He decides that he must visit the Messiah child to see if anything has happened.

Since that first special night, Micah now often visits with young Yeshua. As the father, Joseph, had predicted, the family now lives in the inn itself. As the ancestral home of King David, of which Joseph is a direct descendent, the inn is the perfect residence for Israel's young messiah. After the relative innkeeper learned of the extraordinary events surrounding Yeshua's birth, he had immediately moved the family into the main house, offering up his own room. All had worked out perfectly, to Micah's estimation.

Now out of precaution, the family of King David is keeping the birth of Yeshua a secret. Times are not safe. With the census ordered by the Roman Emperor Augustus, the family knows it is not wise for the Romans to know of Yeshua's birth. In fact, it is the census that initially brought Joseph and his new pregnant bride to Bethlehem. But the shame of Mary being pregnant before the couple was lawfully married banished them to the stable behind the main house that momentous night. Joseph's relatives, being proud of their direct ancestry to King David, did not want the embarrassment to the family name. However, that all changed as soon as the relatives learned of the supernatural events told by the shepherds.

The next day, before Micah could pay Yeshua and his parents a visit, a caravan of regal travelers arrives. Instead of passing through, the caravan sets up camp near the olive grove a short distance from Bethlehem. Micah is at the local oasis watering his family's sheep when servants from the caravan lead their camels over to drink. One of the servants approaches Micah. He is unusually tall, his stature intimidating. He is of dark complexion, his dress clearly that of a foreign country. Yet he speaks Micah's tongue—Aramaic. His masters are priests who have come from the distant land of Persia, he tells Micah, after introducing himself as Belteshazzar. Micah has heard news of the birth of a special child king that would have taken place eight months ago.

Micah's eyes grow wide. He can't hide his surprise. How could this stranger from another country know of Yeshua's birth? Even the time he was born. Especially with Yeshua's identity a closely guarded secret, even locally. He isn't sure how to answer. The eyes of the tall servant are piercing, making Micah feel as if the man is reading his thoughts. Finally, the servant speaks. He should introduce Micah to his masters, who are Magi. They can explain all to Micah and the reason for their traveling here to this village of Bethlehem.

The servant Belteshazzar leads Micah over to the camp, where he introduces the shepherd boy to the Magi. Instead of princes, which their regal appearance resembles, Micah learns they are high priests of a religious order known as Zoroastrianism. Their religion studies the stars for signs, the Magi explain, using Belteshazzar to translate into Aramaic so Micah can understand. Some months back in the spring, a special meeting of planets in the heavens occurred that had never happened. But how would that tell them the Messiah King was born? asks Micah.

Taking the boy into their tent, the Magi unroll charts displaying an arrangement of stars and planets with lines connecting the celestial objects, along with strange mathematical writings, which Micah doesn't understand. The Magi explain. When they observed this special conjunction of planets, to the eye they resembled an extraordinarily bright star. They knew this was the event that the priests before them had anticipated and searched the night sky for a sign for 500 years, finally culminating with the appearance of the star that now announced a special king's birth. It was this star that they had followed for months now. Their journey carried them all the way from Persia.

But how did their religion foretell of this event? asks Micah.

It began during the rule of the great Persian king Cyrus, who had ruled the known world 500 years earlier, to include Israel. The Magi explained to Micah how King Cyrus had become a follower of the Hebrew God Jehovah, following the capture of Babylon, where the Jews were held captive. Cyrus would release the Jews to return to their homeland. As well, the king who had become a friend of the Hebrews, would help rebuild their sacred temple.

Under Cyrus's directive, Zoroastrian priests began to study the Jewish scriptures to understand what the future foretold according to their prophets. Cyrus instructed his priests to follow the teachings of Daniel, the Jewish prophet, who ever since the lion's den, had secured his position with the king. That was how they came to know of a future messiah king prophesied to one day arrive. One even greater than Cyrus.

Along with this prophecy, a star, it was prophesied, would appear out of Judea. A rare conjunction of the planets, along with other events that their study of the heavens revealed. It was the sign that they for so long had looked to appear. It was why they now traveled to Bethlehem.

When the Magi mention the prophet Micah, who foretold how the Messiah King would come from

Bethlehem, Micah is thrilled. He has heard of this prophet in the scriptures, his namesake, but not the connection to Bethlehem. Suddenly, he is overwhelmed with a sense of destiny. First, it was the night of Yeshua's birth, and now the chance meeting these Magi. He must share how he came to meet the child king.

Now it is the Magi's turn to be amazed as Micah shares the extraordinary events of that night around the campfire with his family. When he finishes, they are overjoyed that they have read the signs in the heavens correctly. First, Micah tells the Magi that he must speak to the parents to get permission before revealing the child's whereabouts. Even now, officials know nothing of Yeshua's birth, Micah explains, and it must stay that way. The Magi understand. They have already been warned in a dream that Herod intends the child harm. The dream occurred after they visited the ruler at his palace in Herodium, before proceeding to Bethlehem. Until the dream, they had thought the king was sincere when he had said that he wanted to come worship the child too, like the Magi. Herod is a despot who must never know anything of the child, they declare.

It is best if they visit the child under the cover of darkness, suggests the servant Belteshazzar. They all agree. Micah leaves the priests to decide with Joseph and Mary. Fascinated by the news of these royal visitors, the parents agree for the priests to visit their son later that night. With the rendezvous set up, Micah returns to the Magi's camp to make plans. Belteshazzar, it turns out, has a scheme how to make the rendezvous without anyone the wiser.

Meanwhile, Herod has sent a spy to follow the Magi's caravan and monitor their activity. Being a paranoid despot, Herod trusts no one when it comes to his position ruling the region. Rome allows him to rule because he is ruthless and keeps Judea under control. Rome tolerates no trouble spots in its empire. The spy he has sent, Haman, Herod knows to be one of his shrewdest. Haman himself knows if he is successful on this mission, his reward will allow him to retire to the beaches along the Mediterranean. Now he is keeping a close watch on the Magi's camp from a distance, alert to any movements that might tell him the priests may have found the child. He has noticed the shepherd boy come and go. Something about this alerts Haman's suspicions.

To conceal the rendezvous, Belteshazzar has proposed a bonfire along with exotic entertainment as a distraction. When the bonfire festivities attract the attention of the town, the Magi slip away to visit the child. They have disguised themselves and covered their finery under clothing worn by shepherds. The ploy works as Micah leads the Magi to the Inn.

Legend of the Wooden Star

Joseph and Mary are amazed to hear the story that the Magi have told Micah earlier. That their son's birth has brought these exotic priests from a distant country to pay homage, humbles the couple. And now the priests reveal that they have brought gifts: Rare expensive spices, along with valuable gold. As Mary listens to the Magi tell of the Star's significance in the Scriptures, Mary takes out the wooden star Micah carved. They will treasure these gifts and the priest's visit this night. The Magi take their leave. They will have much to share with their people when they return to Persia, they say. Surely, they have met the King of Kings. The Heavenly events they have heard and seen will forever confirm this.

Later that night, the Magi break camp and stealthily depart the area under the cover of darkness. It isn't until the next morning that the spy Haman realizes he's been duped. Fearful for his life, he rushes back to Herod's palace to tell the king the unwelcome news. Herod is furious and orders the imprisonment of his spy until he can be executed. Now Herod must take extreme measures. He orders his soldiers to Bethlehem, where they will ensure the threat of this child king is removed for good.

That night, as Herod's soldiers make their way to the village, Joseph is warned in a dream of the impending danger. He wakens Mary. Hastily, they slip out of town and head into the countryside. A short distance out of the village, they come to the shepherd's camp. It is Micah's family.

"What is the best way to head south to Egypt?" asks Joseph, explaining the warning he received.

"While the backcountry is rugged, it will make it difficult for anyone to find them," say the shepherds.

"Can he help to guide the child and family out of the area?" Micah asks his father.

"It could be dangerous," cautions his father. Especially when Micah must return alone.

"I will go with Micah," Uncle Reuben offers.

Besides, no one knows the backcountry better than himself. It's the area where Reuben and his band of Zealots set up ambushes for Roman soldiers passing through.

Before they can get far, they see a century of soldiers, numbering at least eighty strong approaching, their torches lighting the area. Reuben hurries them into a nearby olive grove to hide. There, they huddle behind a huge ancient olive tree with heavy low hanging limbs and gigantic gnarled roots roaming above ground. Just as a soldier approaches, the child whimpers. Stricken with fear, Mary tries to quiet him, but the noise has alerted the soldier. His torch illumining the area, they crouch as he starts to make his way around the gnarly roots.

Just then, the tall imposing servant who Micah immediately recognizes to be Belteshazzar, steps into the soldier's path out of nowhere. "Who are you?" the soldier asks menacingly.

In a calm voice, Belteshazzar responds, "I was just passing through."

"Who made that noise?" asks the soldier. "It sounded like a child." Suspicious, the soldier draws his sword.

"No cause for alarm," Belteshazzar replies. "It was a bird taking flight from the big tree."

"No, it was a child's voice," says the soldier. Now he holds the torch close to the tall stranger's face. His anger turns to bewilderment.

"What about this?" says Belteshazzar. He has a gift for the soldier for the fine work they do defending the countryside. He offers the gift of a game the soldiers are renowned for playing, Ludus Latrunculorum. The gift does the trick. As the tall stranger holds out a rolled-up piece of leather, the soldier sheaths his sword and accepts the gift.

"The stranger should leave the area at once," the soldier warns. "Tonight, there will be trouble." With that, he turns and walks off.

Belteshazzar steps around the tree where they are hiding.

"Where did he come from?" asks Micah. He is thrilled to see the servant who he now considers a friend.

Belteshazzar explains how he stayed back after the caravan left, sensing he might be needed. He had stopped by the shepherd's camp. That is how he learned that they were headed south to escape trouble. Belteshazzar is headed in that direction as well. "May I join you?" he asks.

"We are all too happy for your company," says Joseph, thanking the tall foreigner for dealing with the soldier.

By now, the soldiers have finished searching the olive grove and have moved on in the direction of Bethlehem. Belteshazzar has acquired a donkey with a cart close to where they are now. It is tied up waiting, Belteshazzar explains. The news excites and relieves Joseph and Mary. It is an all-night walk by foot to Hebron, which is too much for Mary and the child.

Staying on the back roads, they head to Hebron, through the hill country, to a town where trade routes intersect passing through Palestine. Arriving the next morning, with Belteshazzar's help, Joseph plans for his family to join a caravan of merchants headed into Egypt. To pay for their passage, Joseph uses some of the gold gifted by the Magi. Over the months since Yeshua's birth, Micah has become close with Joseph and

Mary. Mary takes out the wooden star that she carries inside her robe. She promises that will cherish his gift and tell her son all that happened. One day, they will meet again. Micah watches until the caravan carrying the family has disappeared out of sight, Belteshazzar traveling with them. Then Micah and his Uncle Reuben head back.

Late that night, Micah and his uncle arrive back in Bethlehem to horrific news. In the middle of the night, the soldiers they had evaded went door to door, taking any male child who was two years old or younger. The village is traumatized, with mothers wailing and mourning. No one knows the motive for such a cruel act against innocent children. Except for Micah and his uncle, but they are sworn to secrecy. What happened next is excruciating to hear. The soldiers ripped the small children from their mother's arms and carried them off to be slaughtered outside the town. Word has it that the total number of male boys numbered twenty.

Upon hearing this, Reuben and Micah rush back to their family's camp. Micah has a little brother who is not yet two. To his horror, he learns that his brother has suffered the same fate. The family is devastated.

"This cannot be, not after all we witnessed and then did to help the Child King," the grandfather wails. He has ripped his clothes and covered himself in ashes.

There is no answer. No solace. Micah's Uncle Reuben was right. There is no justice, except what a person takes into his own hands.

Now a young teenager, Micah is considered old enough to make his own decisions. That day, he tells his family he is joining his Uncle Reuben's revolutionary group to fight against the tyrants of Israel. Whatever the truth about the child king, Micah's anger is now directed at Heaven. If he cannot trust the God of Abraham, there is no one he can trust but himself. From that day, Micah will grow into a fierce revolutionary, legendary for preying on Roman soldiers occupying the Jew's homeland. Not only does Micah become a folk hero, but he will earn the title of "Most Wanted" by the Romans.

Thirty-three years later . . .

Destiny has another plan for Micah. For once again, Micah will cross paths with the child king. By now Yeshua, also known as Jesus, is a grown man. To the masses who have heard him speak and perform miracles, he is a prophet. Some even proclaim him to be the long-awaited Messiah.

That crossing of paths again happens during the annual Passover celebration in Jerusalem. Jesus has entered the city to much fanfare. So much so that the religious leaders are insane with jealousy and rage at how the crowds esteem him as a prophet, often at their expense, who he accuses of being vipers and hypocrites.

The Jewish leaders have hatched a plot. Already, they have bribed one of his disciples. The trap is set. When Jesus goes to the garden outside of town to pray, the traitor disciple leads a party of Jewish leaders to him, bringing with them an escort of Roman soldiers. They arrest Jesus, then try him twice. Once before the Sanhedrin, a tribunal of Jewish elders, where he is convicted of Blasphemy, bringing a death sentence under Jewish law. Then Jesus is taken before Pontius Pilate with accusations of insurrection, which again, the penalty under Roman law is death.

In the meantime, Pilate's wife has warned him about this prophet. She has had a dream that he is innocent, and if Pilate gets involved in sentencing this man, he will rue the day. Heeding his wife, he sends Jesus to Herod Antipas, who, in turn, wants no part of convicting the prophet, thus angering the Jews he rules. Herod sends Jesus back to Pilate to determine the popular teacher's fate. Now Pilate comes up with what he is certain is a brilliant solution to extricate himself from the whole affair. He will find the prophet guilty of the charges. That will appease Caiaphas and the host of Pharisees and Sadducees pressing for a conviction. Then later that day, Pilate, following his tradition of pardoning a prisoner who is popular with the crowds, will offer to pardon Jesus. Given the prophet's popularity, Pilate is certain the crowds will call for his release. Problem solved.

What happens next is only partly known to history.

Some years earlier, a notorious leader of a revolutionary group known as Zealots, sworn enemies of Roman occupation of the Jew's homeland, has been arrested. Convicted of insurrection, he is condemned to die. Now, three years later, he sits in prison because of his popularity with the Jews. They would revolt if he were ever executed. His name is Barabbas. Pilate decides that now is the opportune time to execute this leader. It will happen when he gives the crowds a choice between their prophet and a revolutionary. Orders are sent to the Pretorian Guard to prepare Barabbas for his execution.

At the allotted time the next day, after a night of putting the prophet on trial, Pilate appears before the crowd with Jesus.

"Is this the man you would see me pardon this day?" he asks the crowd.

The shrewd Caiaphas, learning of Pilate's plan, has placed instigators in the crowd. When Pilate offers Jesus, they began to call out for the release of Barabbas instead. Soon, the whole crowd is calling for the same. It is Jesus they want crucified, not Barabbas!

Finally, Pilate relents and washes his hands in front of the crowd and declares the blood is on their hands, not his.

To that, the crowd cries out, "May his blood be on our hands!"

Barabbas is in his cell awaiting his time when the soldiers arrive to escort him before Pilate. He is unprepared for what happens next. He learns he has been pardoned by Pilate and made a free man. In his stead, the prophet Jesus is to be crucified. He is free to go, he is told, to a cheering crowd. That is, so long as he renounces his revolutionary past. Barabbas, who has had enough of life on the run and hiding, agrees to the conditions of freedom.

From this day, he will take back the name given him at birth—Micah.

Barabbas, meaning Son of the Father, as in Father Abraham, had taken on that name when he became a revolutionary after his younger brother was slaughtered that night by Herod's orders. Now an older and wiser man, he is ready to go back to his family and a life of peace.

Micah's shepherd family is there in Jerusalem. They have traveled to the holy city, like all faithful Jews throughout Palestine and beyond, to be present during this most important Jewish holiday. When they learn that their brother has been released, they meet up with him to celebrate. "Will you return with us?" they ask.

"Yes," Micah says. He is done with his other life.

Then Micah hears the news. His young son, Judah, who is five, is deathly ill with the contagion sweeping through the region claiming the lives of young children. His brothers break the news that Judah may not survive. Micah must hurry home to Judah before it is too late.

Micah has not seen his son for three years. Not since he was ambushed and captured by Roman soldiers. Now, however, he feels compelled to linger. He has heard that a prophet who people are calling the Messiah, whose name is Yeshua, is to be executed in his place. Micah thinks back to the child king of that same name he met those many years ago. In fact, the prophet would be about the same age. Could he be the same person? He must know the answer before he leaves Jerusalem. Especially since this prophet is taking his place of execution.

At noon, Micah follows the crowd outside the city to the place called Golgotha, where the Romans carry out public executions. He works his way to the front of the crowd as the prophet is paraded through the streets while being made to carry his own cross. The man is beaten badly and barely recognizable as a man. When he collapses, Micah rushes forward to help, but a Roman soldier grabs another spectator who is standing closer and orders him to help the condemned prophet carry his cross.

Outside the city, at the place of execution, Micah watches the gripping spectacle. The prophet is innocent of anything wrong, he hears people sobbing. Nearby, he sees a familiar face. It is one of his old Zealot revolutionaries, Simon. Their eyes meet and Simon comes over. Soon he is telling Micah what has happened to his life over the past three years after Micah was captured and imprisoned. Simon soon after became a follower of the prophet, one of Jesus's twelve disciples. Micah can hardly believe his ears. As he asks questions of Simon, he soon confirms this prophet Jesus is Yeshua, the child born that night long ago in Bethlehem.

Micah tells Simon he is not going to believe this, but he was there the night the night Yeshua was born. Simon smiles. He already knows. There is someone he wants Micah to meet. He leads Micah over to a woman, who though matured, is recognizable to Micah. When Micah last saw her, she was only a young girl in her teens. It is Mary, the mother of Yeshua.

She is crying while one of the prophet's disciples comforts her.

"Do you remember me?" Micah asks.

She smiles. "Yes, of course."

Micah finds his eyes start to tear. Meeting Mary, seeing the man who as a child he helped to escape death, and now watching the spectacle, it all is too much.

Mary lays a hand on Micah's arm. "Do not grieve," she says. Jesus told her and all his followers that this must happen. "You see," she tells Micah, "the Kingdom Jesus preached of is not an earthly kingdom. It is a heavenly kingdom." She knows all about the life Micah lived after that night, when the innocent boys were slaughtered by that tyrant Herod. Simon has told her all about Micah becoming Barabbas.

Mary explains, "Just like today, my son has taken the place of Micah on that cross. He is doing the same for all who will follow him. If Micah wants to be a part of a real revolution, he must leave his past life behind and become a follower of my son, like his friend Simon."

At that, Mary removes something from under her cloak. Micah cannot believe what he is seeing. It is the wooden star he carved so many years ago.

"Do you remember how you promised me that you would keep the star close to yourself?"

"I do," she says.

She holds the little wooden star out for Micah to take back. The star he gifted to Baby Yeshua.

"Does the star make you think of something else?" Mother Mary asks.

His eyes go to where Yeshua the prophet hangs. Revelation fills his eyes. "The star resembles the cross where the Messiah now hangs," says Micah.

Mother Mary smiles. "That was the real message brought with the appearing of the Bethlehem Star. Why Yeshua, which means "God with us," had come to earth. Just as that star lit up the sky that night, my son's life was meant to bring light to the world."

As Micah listens, he feels tears fill his eyes. He looks over at the cross where the man he rescued as a child now hangs, nailed to the Roman cross. Just then, Yeshua locks eyes with him. For a long moment, he gazes at Micah, then gives the faintest nod before raising his eyes heavenward. In a moment, Yeshua will breathe his last breath. The torture inflicted by Rome's tyranny is over. Micah feels his own heart stop as he hears the prophet's last agonizing words, "It is over."

At that moment, taking the hand of Mary, he utters a prayer while gazing heavenward. He will commit the rest of his life to be a disciple of Yeshua.

With that, Mary and Micah's old friend Simon welcomes him as a follower of Jesus.

After a sad but joyous moment, Micah tells Mary and his old friend Simon that he must take leave. He has learned that his son is deathly sick, who his family fears may not recover. She will pray for Micah's son,

Mary promises, giving him a hug. After all that Micah has gone through, she has faith that God will grant favor in the name of her own son Jesus and raise up Micah's son off his deathbed.

Encouraged, but still fearful for his son, Micah finds his shepherd family and heads out of Jerusalem to their camp in the outlying countryside. During the journey home that carries into night, Micah finds himself gazing up at the starry night, remembering his time as a young shepherd boy. Of those many quiet nights, when he would study the stars and wonder, he marvels now how he could never have imagined how destiny would bring him to this moment. That he would be present at the birth of the Jew's messiah, helping to save the young child, and now finding that the grown messiah somehow had played a part in saving Micah's own life.

The next morning, having refused to stop to sleep, Micah felt his heart fill with apprehension as he approached the family's camp. It was then he saw his wife, Leah, who he had not seen for three long years, step out of their family's modest home. Spying him in the distance, she Immediately set out at a run to meet him. But what shocked and thrilled Micah at the same time was the young boy running beside her. It was his son, Judah!

As Micah meets his little family, he sweeps his son into his arms, hugging him tightly.

"What happened?" he asks Leah. Last he heard, young Judah was deathly ill.

"It is a miracle." She smiles joyfully, hugging Micah. "It happened yesterday. At the time Judah was delirious with a high fever. I was so fearful that he wouldn't make it through that night. Then his fever suddenly started to subside. By night, his temperature was back to normal, and he was sleeping peacefully. After sleeping soundly all night, he woke this morning totally well."

Micah studies his wife. "What time did Judah start to get better yesterday?" he asks.

She thinks back a moment. "It was about the ninth hour in the afternoon. I still don't understand how his condition could have improved so dramatically. Not with what was happening to so many children his age who weren't so fortunate. I can only surmise that it was a miracle. Like the miracles I have been hearing follow the prophet traveling about Judea proclaiming news that the Kingdom of God has come."

Micah recalls back to yesterday at the site of the crucifixion. That was the hour he had locked eyes with Yeshua, just before the prophet died. Suddenly, Micah feels a joy well up in him he has never experienced.

A joy that makes him gaze upward to heaven, his being filled with gratitude.

Reaching inside his robe, Micah takes out the wooden star. Smiling at his wife, Leah, he nods. "What happened to our son was in fact a miracle. A miracle that began many years ago."

"What do you mean?" asks Leah.

Seeing the wooden star, his son reaches for it, which Micah gives to him.

"Come," says Micah, holding his son while taking his wife's hand and heading to their home, "I have a story to tell you. A story that started with the appearance of a Miracle Star one night many, many years ago."

Play Ends

Part 3
The Miracle

As the last scene played out, the curtains closed. Hunter had watched the entire performance tonight while seated with the audience. Now, soaking in what he just watched, he couldn't be prouder. The performance had gone off flawlessly. The scenes transitioned without a hitch. No gaffs that the audience would pick up on. The crowd's response was immediate too. Not just polite clapping, but a wildly exuberant ovation with everyone standing.

The curtains reopened. This time, with the full cast and crew onstage. They waved and bowed, basking in the applause. Hunter grinned from ear to ear while his Opa patted him on the back and his Oma hugged him. Farther down the pew, Hunter's folks and Aunt Jenny gave him a thumbs-up.

To a director, there was no better rush than an audience's applause. What Mr. Wilson called the final and most important act. Foremost to remember, they were there to entertain. He had reminded the cast of that during his pep talk. The applause was the gauge that measured how well they succeeded in doing that. Hunter turned to study the crowd around him. The people's faces left no doubt that the show had entertained.

Just then, Hunter felt a tap on his shoulder. It was Joey's mother. The look on her face said something was wrong.

"Is Joey okay?" He quickly turned to look where Joey's gurney was parked in the handicap section.

Karen shook her head. "He's fine. It's something else." Her voice was anxious. "It's so startling . . . I don't even know what to believe."

Karen had Hunter concerned now. "Tell me."

She stumbled over her words. "It's about the actor who played the Magi's servant . . ." She paused to get her emotions under control. "Joey recognized him as soon as he entered the auditorium with the Wise Men."

Hunter's eyebrows raised. "You mean Caelum? How would he recognize him? He's never met him." Hunter and Denèe had wanted Caelum to visit Joey at the hospital, but so far, that had not happened.

"I want Joey to tell you that part," she said.

"Okay." Hunter followed Karen up the aisle, back to where Joey was waiting. Now Hunter had the strangest feeling. Reaching the gurney, he saw that the gurney had Joey inclined where he could watch everything. His face wore a scowl.

"Joey, tell me what happened. Your mom says you recognized Caelum?"

Joey shook his head no, "It was Shaz I saw. I keep telling Mom that."

Hunter was confused. "I don't understand."

"Shaz was playing the Magi's servant."

Hunter could see from the boy's expression that Joey believed what he was saying.

What Joey just said felt like a shock. Hunter looked from Joey to Karen. For a moment, he wasn't sure what to say. Getting ahold of himself, he said, "Joey, you realize you are saying that the actor who we had playing Belteshazzar, whose name is Caelum, wasn't Caelum but your hospital friend Shaz?"

Hunter could not believe he was even saying that.

Joey frowned. "All I know is that I saw Shaz. And he was wearing the robe and turban that he always has on when he comes to visit me."

Hunter felt relief. That was it. Joey was seeing the costume and thinking it was his friend Shaz. Hunter smiled. "You're seeing them both in the robes. That's all it is."

Joey shook his head vigorously. "No, it wasn't just what he had on. When he first walked in leading the camel, he gave me a smile."

Just then, Ellen and Max walked up. They could see something was up. "What's happened?" they asked.

Karen quickly explained.

"Wow!" said Max. "This is a shocker."

Ellen turned to Hunter. "What are you thinking?"

Hunter studied the crowded auditorium. People were starting to leave. He was thinking he might spy Caelum. Or Shaz.

He turned back to his Oma. "I'm not sure what happened."

Now Hunter saw that Denèe was heading their way, walking briskly. Sensing something was amiss as she came up, she gave a quizzical look. "Is everything okay?"

Hunter answered, "Denèe, you are not going to believe this."

Always the confident one, she challenged, "Tell me."

"Joey saw his friend Shaz tonight."

Denèe turned to Joey, her eyes surprised. "Really? Here tonight?"

Joey nodded.

Hunter shook his head. "That's only part of it. Joey says it was Shaz playing the part of Belteshazzar."

Denèe glanced over at Karen, her eyes asking if what she was hearing really happened.

Karen nodded. "I was right beside Joey when it took place."

"Joey, could it be the robes Caelum was wearing . . . like what Shaz wears when he visits you?"

Joey looked frustrated. "Nobody ever believes me. It was Shaz."

Denèe walked over to Joey and placed a hand on his arm reassuringly. "I'm sorry, Joey, I believe you."

That brought a smile. "I knew you would, Denèe." His defensiveness gone, Joey's face looked peaceful.

Denèe was quiet a moment. Then looking to Hunter, she said, "This is incredible. At the same time, what Joey is saying explains a lot."

"What do you mean?" Hunter asked.

"Let's discuss it in a bit. Right now, let's go find Caelum." She glanced at Joey. "Or Shaz."

Joey was suddenly excited. "Yes! Can you go find him? I want you to meet him."

Denèe tugged on Hunter. "You know how he always leaves soon as it's over."

Hunter nodded. Denèe had a point. Caelum always left as soon as rehearsal was over. He had done the same with the first two shows. In fact, he didn't stay for the meet & greet social that followed the performances the past two nights.

"You're right," Hunter agreed. Then speaking to the group, "We'll be back shortly. Hopefully, we'll solve this mystery!"

Hunter and Denèe burst into the changing area, out of breath.

"Has anybody seen Caelum?" Hunter called out.

"What did he do?" Miss Cho frowned.

"Nothing, Miss Cho," Denèe answered, "but it's important we find him."

Miss Cho shook her head. "He didn't turn in his costume yet. If you find him, tell him I'm looking for him. "

Barely slowing down, Hunter and Denèe headed to the fellowship hall.

After a few minutes of looking with no results, Hunter summed up the situation. "He's left. Let's go back to join everybody."

Denèe scowled. "Joey will be disappointed."

Heading back to the auditorium, Denèe asked, "What do you make of what Joey said?"

Hunter was thoughtful. "On one hand, it sounds too incredible. Then, I can see where it makes sense.

I mean, look at how Caelum showed up to audition about the same time Joey first arrived at the hospital."

Denèe added, "I always thought there was something strange about how he came to interview for the part. It always felt too coincidental."

Hunter nodded back. "I agree. And knowing so many details about the Wise Men back then."

Denèe continued, "Okay, so if Caelum and Shaz are the same person, then who is he really?"

Hunter looked at his girlfriend and offered a wry smile. "You wanted a Christmas mystery . . . remember? We for sure have walked into one."

Joey's face fell when he saw them coming up the aisle with no Shaz. "You didn't see him, did you?" It wasn't a question. He added, "I knew you wouldn't."

"What do you mean, Joey?" Denèe asked.

Joey shrugged. "I'm not sure. It's like he came from another time."

That got the adults' attention.

Karen spoke, "We're not going to solve anything standing here. Right now, Joey, we have to get you back to the hospital."

Ellen added, "Plus, Max and I brought goodies to enjoy back at Joey's room."

Knowing Joey couldn't stay for the social, Ellen had volunteered to put together refreshments for later.

Hunter spoke, "While you all head to the hospital, Denèe and I want to make an appearance at the party." He looked at Denèe. "Say a few words of thanks to everybody for the incredible work pulling this off."

"It really was spectacular," Ellen added, to nods of agreement.

"Who all is coming?" Max asked, looking at Scott, Ashley, and Jenny. They had joined everyone by now.

"I'm sorry, we can't," Jenny apologized. "I've promised some special treats back home. Plus, it's Christmas Eve. The kids will have to be in bed so Santa doesn't pass by our house." She was speaking to her daughters.

By their expressions, they were not missing what their mom was saying.

Ashley answered, "Scott and I are joining Jenny and the girls back at their house." She looked over at Karen. "Perhaps we can all get together over the holidays? Figure something fun to do. Maybe go ice skating?"

Karen beamed. "That would be wonderful. Especially with the kids close to the same age."

The four children who were talking among themselves cheered at the idea.

Al walked up. By now, he was finished with his sound booth duties. Seeing Hunter and Denèe, the first thing he did was praise the performance. "You guys hit it out of the park tonight."

"Thanks to your work in the sound booth," Hunter and Denèe answered.

Sensing something was up, Al stared at the group and asked, "Did I miss anything?"

Karen answered, "I was planning to tell you later, Al." Now she quickly explained what happened.

Al studied his son. "Joey, you're certain it was your midnight visitor?" He still referred to Shaz by that.

"I'm certain, Dad." Joey's look was firm.

Al accepted what his son said. "I knew there had to be a connection between this so-called Game of Mercenaries showing up in Joey's room and this play."

"You were spot on," said Max.

Ellen added, "We all have questions as to what's going on. Meantime, Karen's right, Joey needs to get back to the hospital."

While the Filipino nurse's aide, who went by the name Sol, wheeled Joey out to the ambulance, Max and Ellen headed to their vehicle, and Hunter and Denèe to the social.

Exiting the church through the front doors, they were hit with a blast of chilly air.

"Brrr." Karen shivered. "Sol, let's hurry up and get Joey into the ambulance."

The ambulance was already idling under the portico.

Joey suddenly spoke, "Mom, Dad, the stars are out! I have to look for my miracle star." His voice was pleading.

Al and Karen both gazed up at the sky. He was right. During the performance, the clouds had broken up, so now the sky was clear and the stars were at their brightest.

Karen looked at Al. "We need to take a minute so Joey can look for his star."

Hesitant at first, Al finally nodded, then speaking to Joey, "We need to make it quick, son. With your weak defenses, you could catch pneumonia out here."

It's what the doctors had worried about all along.

Sol rolled the gurney out from under the portico into the open sky.

His face excited, Joey searched the sky. "Shaz said to look on the horizon—in the direction where the sun sets."

"That would be over there." Al pointed.

Maggie and Alex now joined their brother to see.

"Is that it?" Maggie pointed.

Sure enough, an extraordinarily large star, even bigger than a planet, hung close to the horizon. According to astrologers, by tomorrow night, the two planets would pass and no longer give the effect of a giant star.

"That's it." Joey whispered. "That's the miracle star!"

Tears came to Karen's eyes as she gazed at the rapturous expression on her son's face. It was a look of hope that one could not mistake. She looked at Al, who nodded. He too saw it.

Joey looked at his folks. "I finally found it! Now I know my miracle will come."

Karen smiled a smile bigger than she had for a long time. "We believe so too, Joey."

"We should really go now," Sol spoke up. He had stayed with Joey dutifully the whole time. "It's too cold for him to stay out here. I would be in trouble if the doctors knew—"

"I'm okay now, Sol," Joey said, still gazing at the phenomenon. "I found my miracle star."

A half-hour later, the ambulance transporting Joey pulled under the hospital's covered entrance. Behind the ambulance, Al had followed in the SUV with the kids. Sol unloaded the gurney, then wheeled Joey into the reception area. Karen, who had ridden with Joey, found Ellen and Max waiting in the nearby visitor's section.

"Sorry for the delay," she explained. "Don't know whether you noticed, but the stars are finally out tonight. I'll let Joey share what he discovered." Her glowing face told them that the news was exciting.

"We want to hear!" said Ellen.

She and Max followed Karen out to where Joey was waiting. By now, Al and the kids were there too.

"Joey, we want to hear the exciting news!" said Ellen excitedly.

Looking tired from the outing, Joey managed to smile. "I saw the star Shaz told me I needed to discover." His face looked peaceful. "Now I know my miracle will happen."

"Excellent, Joey, we're excited too," said Max, patting the boy's shoulder.

Ellen turned to Karen. "What do you say we go up to Joey's room to get the refreshments laid out?"

Max looked at his phone. "Hunter just texted. He and Denèe are on the way here. About ten minutes away."

Over at the nurse's station, Nurse Shelley saw them exit the elevator.

They already heard that she was sacrificing her Christmas Eve to be here for when Joey got back from the play. She gave them a wave.

"How was the play? I want to hear all about it," she gushed.

Joey offered his favorite nurse a big smile. "It was super cool. Especially the camel! Guess what?"

"What?" the nurse answered, leaning over the counter to get closer to the gurney.

"My friend Shaz was at the church tonight."

"What! You're kidding!" The nurse looked at the adults for confirmation.

Karen smiled. "It's true."

"He was in the play," Joey added.

Nurse Shelley's eyes lit up. "Now that's a story I want to hear!"

"We are still trying to understand what it all means," said Karen.

Ellen spoke, "Soon as we get refreshments set up in Joey's room, Nurse Shelley, we want you to come by. And please invite any staff on duty tonight. I brought enough goodies for everyone!"

"I'll be there," the nurse beamed and shot Joey a wink. "I want to hear all about tonight."

Al said to Sol, "I can get Joey to his room. I'm guessing you want to get home to your family."

Sol nodded. "Yes, thank you."

Karen walked over and gave the elderly Filipino a hug. "Thank you, Sol. Merry Christmas."

Al guided the gurney to Joey's room. As they entered, Joey was the first to notice. He pointed at the window. "Look!"

Hanging in place of the gold foil star dangled a small wooden star.

"It's the wooden star from the play!"

"Well, I'll be . . ." Al muttered.

Everyone quickly crowded into the room to see.

Hunter and Denèe, who had just arrived, hurried over to get a closer look.

"Can you take it down so I can see it?" Joey asked.

"Of course," they said.

While Al moved Joey from the gurney to his regular bed, Denèe and Hunter retrieved the star.

"Who could possibly have hung the star while we were gone?" Karen wondered aloud.

"It was my friend Shaz," Joey said confidently.

Legend of the Wooden Star

Holding the star, Joey looked at Hunter and Denèe. "Could this be the star Micah carved?"

Before either could answer, there was a knock at the door.

"Hello, everybody!" It was Dr. Ellie walking in. "Joey, I heard you were back." She smiled at the group. "Along with your fans. How was the play?"

Joey offered a big grin. "It was great!"

Ellen added, "The performance really was awesome, Dr. Ellie. Such an inspiring story. Wish you could have been there." Ellen shot Hunter a proud look. "The audience loved it. Gave a standing ovation."

"That's wonderful." Dr. Ellie smiled. "I have some wonderful news too."

She walked over to get close to Joey. "You know how your donor match changed their mind?"

Joey offered a disappointed look. "Yes."

"That was such disappointing news for all of us." Without stopping, she continued, "I just got word from the International Donor Bank that he's had a change of heart. He's agreed to have the procedure."

"That's a definite?" Al asked protectively, clearly not wanting to see Joey disappointed again.

Dr. Ellie nodded, she understood his concern. "I asked that too, Mr. Haskins. The people I talked to in the Netherlands gave me details not normally shared. Seems this donor lost a grandson to leukemia a year ago after no donor came through. He was bitter until something happened tonight to change his mind. Something about a wooden star and that he was doing it for his grandson."

Looks exchanged at the mention of the wooden star.

The room was quiet while everyone tried to digest what was happening.

"So, what's next?" Al asked.

Dr. Ellie checked her watch. "According to what I was told and because of the urgency, the procedure is scheduled for Tuesday, right after Christmas."

Karen wanted to know more. "What happens then?"

Dr. Ellie explained, "Here's the process. First, a sample of the donor's bone marrow is surgically extracted from his hip. Then from the bone marrow, what's called hematopoietic stem cells, are sourced. Those stem cells will then be transported here."

Dr. Ellie offered Joey an encouraging smile. "Those healthy stem cells will replace your unhealthy blood cells. The process is comparable to a blood transfusion. The new stem cells can then begin to create the healthy bone marrow that your body needs."

Joey gazed at his young doctor, his eyes full of trust.

"So how do the stem cells get from the Netherlands to here?" asked Karen.

Dr. Ellie nodded. "Good question. That's the next important step. Once the stem cells are collected, the material is frozen, then flown directly here."

Dr. Ellie checked her watch, looking hopeful. "Amsterdam is six hours ahead of us. I was told that we should see it by Tuesday night our time."

Dr. Ellie spoke to Joey now. "You've already been through the hard part. All the chemo to get your body ready. Once we do the transfusion, you will start to get well again."

At that, everyone clapped.

Now Denèe asked the question they all were wondering. "Dr. Ellie, you said the donor told them a wooden star changed his mind?"

Dr. Ellie shrugged. "I didn't understand that part. It was such a strange statement. Then I remembered that's the title of your play."

"Not just the play." Joey showed Dr. Ellie the wooden star he was still holding.

"What's that?" she asked.

"My friend Shaz brought this to my room while I was at the play."

The resident doctor gazed at the star with a look of surprise. "May I see it?"

Joey handed it to her. "Pretty cool, right, Dr. Ellie?"

Examining the star, she suddenly stopped. "What did you say was the name of the shepherd boy in your play?"

"Micah," Joey said, looking at Hunter and Denèe, who both nodded.

"Did you see the letters carved on the backside of the star?" Dr. Ellie held up the star for everyone to see. Carved into the back of the star, along the long point, were letters. Unrecognizable.

"I saw them," said Joey. "What do they mean?"

"Those are Hebrew letters," she smiled. "Being Jewish and raised in Israel, I learned Hebrew as a young girl."

"What's it spell?" Joey asked.

Everyone held their breath, waiting.

Dr. Ellie spelled out each letter, first in Hebrew
מִיכָה

Then she repeated in English. "The letters are *M-K-H*."

Legend of the Wooden Star

"What's that mean?" Joey scrunched his face, not understanding.

Dr. Ellie smiled; she understood. "In the Hebrew alphabet, there are no vowels—like *i* or *a*. So, for anyone who understands Hebrew, they know to add the vowels in. When you do that, it spells the name Mikha. Or in English, you would say Micah."

"I knew it!" Joey's face lit up. "That's the name of the shepherd boy."

The room was quiet. Everyone was trying to make sense of what they just heard.

Denèe took Hunter's hand, leading them over to the window. That's when she noticed the book resting on the windowsill.

She picked it up. "Look what somebody brought back." Denèe held up the antique leather-bound *Legend of the Wooden Star*.

Hunter noticed first. "Looks like somebody inserted a note."

Denèe took it out and examined it. "It's addressed to you, Joey."

"Can you read it out loud, please?" he asked.

Denèe began . . .

"Young Joey, the wooden star I've left in your room is a reminder of the real miracle star. The same star that guided the Wise Men to find the baby Jesus. Never forget, faith is believing in something even when we can't yet see it... A miracle happens when it finally appears. It was fun to see you at the play tonight. Hunter and Denèe will explain everything.

Your friend, Shaz"

Now Dr. Ellie confessed what she was thinking, her voice faltering. "I have to admit, I had lost faith seeing the situations every day with children struggling to survive." She offered Joey a tender smile. "Tonight has shown me I can believe again."

Karen spoke, "Dr. Ellie, we are grateful for the care you've given Joey through all this." Al nodded his agreement.

"We are too," said Max and Ellen.

"What will you do with the wooden star?" Denèe asked Joey.

He thought a minute. "I want to hang it back in the window. That way, the next boy or girl who gets my room has their miracle already waiting to happen."

Legend of the Wooden Star

Ellen walked over to the bags she had brought and started setting out the refreshments. "Who's ready for some delicious Christmas cheer?"

"We all are," said Joey.

That brought a round of cheers and a Merry Christmas to all!

The End